CREATED IN DARKNESS
BY TROUBLED AMERICANS

CREATED
IN DARKNESS
BY TROUBLED
AMERICANS

The Best of
McSWEENEY'S
Humor Category

With Introductions by
Harry Magnan, Exalted Ruler of Elks Lodge #3,
and Dave Eggers

EDITED BY
Dave Eggers • Kevin Shay • Lee Epstein
John Warner • Suzanne Kleid

ALFRED A. KNOPF • NEW YORK • 2004

THIS IS A BORZOI BOOK
PUBLISHED BY ALFRED A. KNOPF

Copyright © 2004 by McSweeney's

www.aaknopf.com
www.mcsweeneys.net
Knopf, Borzoi Books, and the colophon are registered
trademarks of Random House, Inc.

Library of Congress Cataloging in Publication Data
Created in darkness by troubled Americans :
the best of McSweeney's humor category / edited by
Dave Eggers . . . [et al.] ; with introductions by Harry
Magnan and Dave Eggers.— 1st ed.
              p.   cm.
           ISBN 1-4000-4224-0
  1. American wit and humor.   I. Eggers, Dave.
              II. McSweeney's
            PN6165.C74 2004
            817'.5408—dc22
              2004004272

Manufactured in the United States of America
First Edition

CONTENTS

FOREWORD

"WE ALL KNOW that there's a specific piece of information in question here. And with regard to it, let me first state that I know you all would like for me to say what we all think I'm coming before you to say. I would like to make it very clear, however, that I do not intend to say it. In addition, I will neither confirm nor deny it. So now that we all understand each other, are there any questions?"

The spokesperson in "The Briefing," a one-act play featured in this collection, refuses to supply the usual clichés; I hope in this foreword to avoid the same calamity. I was asked to write this foreword by a group of openhearted and truly funny people who believe humor and charity go hand in hand. The Benevolent and Protective Order of Elks was formed by actors with just such values. Those values are proudly displayed at San Francisco Lodge #3, the oldest continuously operating lodge in Elkdom.

* * *

Just as this book is a collection of short, funny vignettes, San Francisco Lodge #3 is a rich panoply of individuals supporting a wide array of charities. Among the outside charities and groups supported by San Francisco Lodge #3 are San Francisco Youth Employment Coalition, Big Brothers/Big Sisters, Girl Scouts, Boy Scouts, Cub Scouts, Mission Children, Adolescent and Family Service Center, Rebuilding Together, Edgewood Center for Children and Families, San Francisco Girl's Chorus, and the Rose Resnick Lighthouse for the Blind and Visually Impaired. Additionally, the lodge also awards scholarships for a high school art contest and two essay contests. An equal variety of written humor awaits you in this tome, including plays, mock interviews, pseudo-advertising, and stories all designed to gently poke fun at the American experience while providing a little levity.

Erma Bombeck observed, "Where humor goes, there goes civilization." Each of us provides small activities that increase the livability of our city. This book is one example of a small action that drives us to wink, smile, and chuckle, a short, small respite that brings warmth and belonging to our lives and the lives of those around us. On behalf of San Francisco Lodge #3, of the Benevolent and Protective Order of Elks, congratulations on a wonderful book, and many thanks for the opportunity to pen the foreword.

Harry Magnan
President, San Francisco Lodge #3
Benevolent and Protective Order of Elks

INTRODUCTION

FROM THE BEGINNING, *McSweeney's* has brokered an awkward alliance between two opposing forces. On the one hand, the journal sought to publish experimental fiction and journalism; on the other hand, we hoped to make a home for stories that were funny without being humorous. Though our dream was that these two forces could act as one, as allies and not combatants, this dream was made of stone, or something like petrified wood. Then it turned to ashes. Yet before it turned to ashes it became embers, burning dimly, like a dying fire. Then, once it was ashes, we had no more hope for our dreams, for they were now ashen. Our dreams were no more. We had woken up from our dream, which was a flightless bird.

You have no doubt heard of the many battles, squabbles, fights, and slap-sessions between these two camps. Always this animosity was fueled by those who said that any possibility of peace between two opposites—serious fiction and less serious humor-type writing—was not only impossible, but perhaps not even possible. They said that humor writing should be on the back pages of magazines, and never over 800 words. They said that fiction should never allow one to laugh. And what did we say to that, after thinking about it for a few days and wishing we had had a quicker comeback? We said Nay! We said Nay, these things could coexist, and length need not be an object. Then we hedged a bit, and said, Length is an object, if said pieces are published on the Web, where reading at great length can cause eye strain. And thus was born the idea that sometimes *McSweeney's* would publish funny things— sometimes in the journal, more often on the website—and that said publishing would not mean that *McSweeney's* was always this thing or always that thing. We could publish both sorts of things, sometimes side by side, and often near articles about goats producing spider silk in their milk. But, we said, with heavy heart and fists of fury, we shall never publish poetry.

So then why, you ask—if our goal was to put these things together, less-serious and serious, to dignify one and undignify the other—have we made a collection only of the funny bits? Why remove the stars from the stripes, the Wynonna from the Ashley? The fault is theirs, the people of Denmark. And for this last insult we pledge eternal damnation upon the smug suckholes who call themselves Danes.

What you see here, friends, is some of the best writing our contributors have created while trying to be less serious and being paid very little or nothing. It will fill you with such joy that you may want to beat your head on a rock in the garden. We encourage you to do this, and to never stop dreaming, even if your dreams turn to birds which cannot fly, or which burn up in flight, as if hit by buckshot. Hunting is awesome.

Dave Eggers
Editor, McSweeney's

CREATED IN DARKNESS
BY TROUBLED AMERICANS

A BRIEF PARODY OF A
TALK SHOW THAT FALLS APART
ABOUT HALFWAY THROUGH

Tim Carvell

[BUSY MUSIC AND *a kaleidoscope of colorful graphics, which ultimately part to reveal an ecstatic audience consisting largely of middle-aged women, with some middle-aged men and college students thrown in.*]

HOST
[*standing in the audience, holding a fuzzy-headed, slightly oversized microphone*]
Hello, and welcome back to our show. Our topic today is: "People Who Enjoy Being Verbally Abused by Talk-Show Audiences." Now, before we went to the break, we were talking to Steve.

[*Cut to Steve. He is around thirty-five, about forty pounds overweight, and wearing an unflattering sweater.*]

HOST

Now, Steve: Since you were a teenager, you've fantasized about being told off by a sassy woman holding a microphone. Is that right?

STEVE

[*ashamed*]

Yes. That's right. It's ruined many of my relationships: I can't relate to women unless they have a microphone in their hand and are making disparaging comments about me, preferably in front of a large crowd. Some women tried to accommodate me for a while—we'd attend open-mic nights, high-school football games, companies' annual meetings—any place where there was an audience and a mic, but after a while, none of them would be able to take it anymore.

HOST

Well, we have someone here who wants to comment on that.

SASSY LADY

Yeah, I just wanted to say that you're sick. [*Audience cheers.*] What kind of a man does that to a woman? You need to get yourself some help.

HOST

Steve?

STEVE

[*Looks pleased. Then ashamed. Then pleased.*]

HOST

We have someone else here who'd like to make a comment. Yes, sir?

AUTHORIAL VOICE

Yeah, I think that this is pretty much a one-joke story.

HOST

True enough.

AUTHORIAL VOICE

So, you know, perhaps it could end now.

HOST

Seems fair enough to me.

> [*STEVE, HOST, SASSY LADY begin filing toward the exits of the studio, along with the rest of the audience.*]

AUTHORIAL VOICE

You know, we don't all have to get up and leave. The illusion that any of us actually exists—which was pretty shaky to begin with—has by now been fairly well destroyed. The story can now just end abruptly at any moment.

HOST

True enough. It could just end, cutting either one of us off in mid sen—

   —tence.

AUTHORIAL VOICE

Hm. That's odd. I thought it was going to end just then.

HOST

Yeah. Me too.

[*They stand together, uncomfortably, awaiting the end of the story. A few minutes pass. Then centuries pass. Then a few more minutes. They turn into marvelous fire-breathing dragons, then into baby chicks. They turn one another inside out. They invent time travel, and prevent the assassination of Archduke Franz Ferdinand, only to discover that*

World War I was inevitable, and that nothing in the present day has changed. They introduce the unicorn to the rainforest. A few more centuries pass. They share a hard-boiled egg. Centuries, centuries. Millennia. The story, at long last, ends. No, wait—they also dive for undersea treasure!]

THE SPIRIT OF CHRISTMAS

Kurt Luchs

My dear Mr. Vanderwoude,

Thank you for your recent gift. Now once again as the holidays approach we ask you to remember the plight of the Bosnian and Serbian orphans. For many of these children there will be no Christmas—no presents, no toys, and worst of all no parents to love and protect them. We thank you for your past generosity and hope you will not forget these little ones as you enjoy the comfort and affluence of your safe, warm home during this joyous season.

Yours sincerely,
Kurt Luchs

P.S. Please accept the enclosed paper Christmas wreath, hand-constructed by seven-year-old burn victim Susie, and hang it on your tree. I trust you'll think of the orphans whenever you look at it.

Dear Mr. Vanderwoude,

If this letter happens to cross yours in the mail, please forgive me; I know the post office is slow and unreliable during the Christmas rush. I'm sure you received my last letter and that your generous gift is already on its way to help the homeless orphans of war-torn Bosnia-Herzegovina. But just in case our letter—or even yours, God forbid—might have gone astray, I'm sending this reminder to thank you for what you have already done and to ask if you can find it in your heart to do just a little bit more this Christmas.

Yours sincerely,
Kurt Luchs

P.S. The attached miniature pinecone, painted holiday green and dipped in glitter, was brought back from the former war zone in the tattered coat pocket of a little boy we call Buster. Enjoy.

*   *   *

Dear Mr. Vanderwoude,

I'll admit I'm puzzled. Surely you must have received my previous letters asking you to add just a little holiday cheer to the lives of our orphaned Bosnian and Serbian boys and girls. And surely you cannot be unmoved by their tragic plight—after all, you made a significant contribution to our cause only a few months ago. Perhaps you yourself have faced unfortunate circumstances recently—a long illness, the loss of a job, or even the loss of a loved one. If so, I offer you my deepest, most heartfelt sympathy, and I look forward to hearing from you in the near future when things are going better for you.

But if you are not facing hard times, Mr. Vanderwoude, if what you suffer from is merely a hard heart ... God help you, Mr. Vanderwoude.

Yours,
Kurt Luchs

P.S. The enclosed sketch of the dove of peace was done by little Amalric, a paraplegic war orphan who has learned to draw by holding a piece of charcoal between his teeth. I hope it fills you with the generous spirit of Christmas.

*   *   *

Mr. Vanderwoude,

As I write this, the orphans are weeping. I had to tell them that there would be no toys this Christmas, that they might not even have a roof over their heads come December 25th. "Why?" they cried. "Because a man named Richard Vanderwoude has apparently decided that your unimaginable pain doesn't matter," I said. "Because he has put his own selfish whims and desires above your basic needs. Because he thinks you are not worth saving." At that point I had to restrain one of the children, Tedescu, from leaping through a plate-glass window.

How can I be so sure of your lack of charity? You see, Mr. Vanderwoude, I did a little checking around. I found that you are not sick, that none of your friends or loved ones have died recently, and that you have not only not been fired but have received a substantial raise and promotion in the past few months.

I am not enclosing a postpaid return envelope with this letter because if you do decide to melt your icy heart and send a donation (which I doubt), I think it appropriate that you should pick up the tab.

Yours,
Kurt Luchs

P.S. The enclosed finger painting portrait of you (you're the one with the fangs) is by Lisel, an eight-year-old deaf-mute. The bright object underneath you is either a holiday candle or the flames of Hell. Of course, we can't ask Lisel, can we?

Mr. Vanderwoude,

If you think you can escape the consequences of your evil actions (or rather, inactions) you are wrong. You will pay. I will see to it personally. And I'll have lots of help. You forget, Mr. Vanderwoude, that these are Bosnian and Serbian orphans. They have been handling firearms and explosives since they were two. They are really pissed off at the world and don't know who to blame, but you make a very plausible target. We know where you live.

Kurt Luchs

P.S. The fiery red composition I've attached to this letter is the joint effort of Tommy and Tony, identical twins who have sworn a sacred blood oath (that's their blood on the paper) not to rest until they have taken vengeance upon you. The artwork depicts your head as it would look after a losing encounter with a fragmentation grenade—a picture I hope to see some-day in real life.

*   *   *

O Ricky boy,

You've really done it now, mister. I heard the cops coming up the stairs and managed to hide in an air vent while they ran-sacked my office. After they left I took the few weapons they had missed, stuffed my remaining files into a briefcase, and then torched the place.

So now you know there are no orphans—Bosnian, Serbian, or Martian. But that doesn't let you off the hook, Rick. Not by a long shot. If there had been any orphans, they would have been just as hungry and hopeless as my letters made out, and you'd be just as guilty. Oh no, Vanderwoude, you aren't out of the woods yet. Because no matter where you go or how much police protection they give your worthless ass, I'll find you, I'll hunt you down like a dog and show you ethnic cleansing like you've never seen before.

If I were you I'd start drinking gallon jugs of double espresso right now and make plans to never, ever go to sleep again. Better install rearview mirrors on your glasses, too. Wherever you are, I'll be right behind you.

Kurt Luchs

P.S. Enclosed is an artist's rendering of the place I'd most like to visit on this earth: your grave.

THE BRIEFING:
A PLAY IN ONE ACT
Stuart Wade

SPOKESPERSON
We all know that there's a specific piece of information in question here. And with regard to it, let me first state that I know you all would like for me to say what we all think I'm coming before you to say. I would like to make it very clear, however, that I do not intend to say it. In addition, I will neither confirm nor deny it. So now that we all understand each other, are there any questions?

REPORTER ONE
Will you say what we want you to say?

SPOKESPERSON
Not exactly as you would have me say it. [*Pointing to REPORTER TWO*] Yes—over there?

REPORTER TWO
Is the thing we all want you to say, in fact, true?

SPOKESPERSON

I'm not saying if it is or it isn't. It would be premature to judge that.

REPORTER THREE

Since you're not saying the precise thing we all want you to say, will you say it, but in a slightly different way?

SPOKESPERSON

You mean in a way that would have the same meaning as the way you would all want me to say it?

REPORTER THREE

That is correct.

SPOKESPERSON

I'm not prepared at this time to do that. [*Making eye contact with REPORTER FOUR*] Yes?

REPORTER FOUR

If you won't say what we all would like you to say, or if you won't say it in a slightly different way, will you at least say one or a couple of parts of what we all want you to say?

SPOKESPERSON

If there is a situation where it would become prudent for me to say part or parts of what you all want me to say, I would, yes. But now is not the time.

REPORTER FIVE

When will it be time?

SPOKESPERSON

I don't know the answer to that. I wanted to add something at this point, before we continue. There are some people involved behind the scenes with this thing who deserve to be recognized for all their hard work. This thing has been a team effort all the way, and thanks to them, a real win-win situation as well. [*Pointing to REPORTER SIX*] Yes, go ahead.

REPORTER SIX

This information that we all want you to disclose—might one of us be able to trick you into divulging what we all want you to say?

SPOKESPERSON

If I am slow-witted at that moment, or if I'm not being too careful in choosing my words right then, and if one of you people displays extremely shrewd questioning skills, then yes, it is possible. [*Shielding his eyes*] Yes—all the way in the back there ... you, Miss.

REPORTER SEVEN

I think I know the information we all want you to say but that you aren't saying, and here it is. [*She says something inaudible*] Isn't that right?

SPOKESPERSON

[*Angrily*] Do you expect me to answer that? Next question.

REPORTER EIGHT

When can we expect you to say what we all want you to say?

SPOKESPERSON

Relatively soon.

REPORTER EIGHT

Can you be more specific?

SPOKESPERSON

Well, we are expediting this process, so I would imagine sooner than you might think, but I don't want to mislead any of you as to exactly when. [*Indicating silver-haired woman seated in front row of media*] Yes, Helen?

REPORTER NINE

I heard some experts giving their opinions about the information we all want you to say. Can you respond to these expert comments?

SPOKESPERSON

Well, I can't speculate on others' comments. And I'm not an expert. [*Looks up to assembled throng*] I have time for one more question. In the middle there, yes—you sir? [*Points to bearded man standing in center of group*]

REPORTER TEN

Might I interject a witty comment at this juncture to break up the tension? [*Says something inaudible*]

[*Everyone laughs*]

Curtain.

ON THE IMPLAUSIBILITY
OF THE DEATH STAR'S
TRASH COMPACTOR
J. M. Tyree

I MAINTAIN THAT the trash compactor on board the Death Star in *Star Wars* is implausible, unworkable, and, moreover, inefficient.

The Trash Compactor Debate turns on whether the Death Star ejects its trash into space. I, for one, believe it does. Though we never see the Death Star ejecting its trash, we do see another Empire ship, the so-called Star Destroyer, ejecting its trash into space. I therefore see no reason to suspect that Empire protocol dictating that trash be ejected into space would not apply equally to all Empire spacecraft, including the Death Star.

The Death Star clearly has a garbage-disposal problem. Given its size and massive personnel, the amount of waste it generates—discarded food, broken equipment, excrement, and the like—boggles the imagination. That said, I just cannot fathom how an organization as ruthless and efficiently run as the Empire would have signed off on such a dangerous, unsanitary, and shoddy garbage disposal system as the one depicted in the movie.

Here are the problems, as I can ascertain them, with the Death Star's garbage-disposal system:

1. Ignoring the question of how Princess Leia could possibly know where the trash compactor is, or that the vent she blasts open leads to a good hiding place for the rescue crew, why are there vents leading down there at all? Would not vents leading into any garbage-disposal system allow the fetid smell of rotting garbage, spores, molds, etc., to seep up into the rest of the Death Star? Would not it have been more prudent for the designers of the Death Star to opt for a closed system, like a septic tank?

2. Why do both walls of the trash compactor move toward each other, rather than employing a one-movable-wall system that would thus rely on the anchored stability, to say nothing of the strength, of the other, nonmoving wall, to crush trash more effectively?

3. Why does the trash compactor compact trash so slowly, and with such difficulty, once the resistance of a thin metal rod is introduced? Surely metal Death Star pieces are among the main items of trash in need of compacting. It thus stands to reason that the trash compactor should have been better designed to handle the problem of a skinny piece of metal. (And while I hate to be the sort of person who says I told you so, I'd be remiss if I didn't point out that a one-movable-wall system would have improved performance.)

4. Why does the trash compactor only compact trash sideways? Once ejected into space, wouldn't the flattened, living-room-sized, and extremely solid panes of trash that result from such a primitive, unidirectional trash compactor pose serious hazards for Empire starships in the vicinity?

5. And what of the creature that lives in the trash compactor? Presumably, the creature survives because the moving walls do not extend all the way to the floor of the room, where the liquid is. After all, if the walls reached the floor, the creature would be killed each time trash is compacted. The design employed on the Death Star must allow the organic trash to filter down to the bottom, where the parasitic worm-creature devours it. But what happens when heavier pieces of non-organic trash fall down there? Would such trash not get wedged under the doors, causing them to malfunction? Do storm troopers have to confront the creature each time they retrieve pieces of uncompacted trash?

6. Why not have separate systems for organic and inorganic waste, thus allowing full compaction of the inorganics and a closed sanitary system for the organics?

7. Why does the Empire care, anyway, about reducing its organic garbage output? Are we to believe that the architects of the Death Star, a group of individuals bent on controlling the entire known universe, are also concerned about environmental issues? Would organic garbage rot in space? So what? Furthermore, why has the Empire gone to the trouble of acquiring a frightening parasitic worm-creature and having it eat all organic trash, especially given the aforementioned flaws in the design of the compactor and overall maintenance hassles?

8. Personally, were it up to me, I would have designed special garbage ships instead of employing a crude, cumbersome, and inefficient (to say nothing of unsanitary) compactor-worm combo to deal with the trash.

9. If the Empire insists on ejecting trash into space, why bother compacting it? Space is infinite, is it not? In such an environment, it hardly matters what size the trash is. In fact, a persuasive argument can be made that it's actually better for

the trash to take up more space, so that it appears on radar systems as something for Empire ships to avoid. Compacted trash creates smaller chunks of harder trash that would undoubtedly cause serious damage to Empire starships. And needless to say, damage to starships would, in turn, create yet more hassles and headaches for the Empire.

Please understand, gentle reader, I am all for creating hassles and headaches for the Empire. I just doubt that the Empire would have created so many for itself. Q.E.D.

PREVIEW OF SUMMER CAMPS
Jeff Johnson

Camp Tickles

Located thirty-two miles south of Akron, OH, on County Trunk R, Camp Tickles is essentially a clown camp for clown prodigies ages 7 to 11. While clowning and clownlike activities take up the lion's share of camp time, Camp Tickles is also a self-esteem-boosting "challenge camp." Challenge One involves the cabins, which are constructed in the camp kitchen and the camp's great lawn over the first few days and are freestanding structures made of marshmallow and sticks. Campers (in groups of five) do not and will not sleep until they have baked and sculpted their own cabins. Blueprints are provided by counselors on the first day of camp. Challenge Two involves the refurbishing and restoration of several turn-of-the-century coin-operated (nickels) games in the "Coney Island" style. Campers (in groups of forty-three) will liberally apply sunscreen, then ride on the back of eastern-bound flatbed trucks to Camp Tickles's warehouse near Coney Island in New York, where they will be given several tools and instructions. Some Internet searches for older instruction manuals will be conducted, and some direction will be provided by Lloyd McAfee, restoration specialist. Challenge Three involves hole-patching of several Ohio roads and adjacencies. Campers (in groups of three) will be provided with red wagons, tar, shovels, levels, and maps of pothole-riddled areas, most of which are within a fourteen-mile radius of Camp Tickles. Campers should ask area farmers and business owners for water, or bring canteens. Campers will be rewarded for completing challenges at a ceremony in the last week of camp.

Camper's Checklist:
1. Two bedsheets (one to use while the other is at the laundry facility).
2. Clown makeup.
3. Clown costume.
4. $70 in singles.
5. One towel.
6. Canteen (optional).
7. Knife.
8. Swimsuit.
9. Tweezers.
10. Magic Marker.
11. Phone card.
12. Ace bandages.
13. Matches.
14. Sunscreen.
15. Cookies.
16. Bratwurst.
19. Tennis balls (juggling).
20. Parachute.
21. Aspirin.

Camp Tickles runs from June 1 to August 8. $539.

S-MEGA Camp
June 15–July 30
Weekly sessions $349
Concordia, MN

Taped to lockers at St. Cloud High School, May 22, 2000:

Hey Gang:

Mr. Weeshof here again. I know, I know you're ready for summer vacation to kick in. Well, guess what? Me too. But this is just a note about what I have been mentioning since, oh, I don't know, last fall!!! And it is for achievers, and more importantly S-MEGA (Sales and Marketing Education Groups of America) Achievers and Strivers (of all levels). Gang, frankly, some of you worked hard this year, and some of you, well, just came to class. No big whoop, but for S-MEGA achievers— i.e., the kids who really want to take it to the next level, the kids who sold, and sold, and sold Chippie mascot sweatshirts, T-shirts, and power towels when our wrestlers went to state; to the kids who saw what was going on with the Tart N' Tiny inventory and acted swiftly and accordingly; the kids who got the plaque from David Zanyrton at Beich's promotional chocolates division for all the sales of their CRISP, CARAMEL, and MILK CHOCOLATE bars due to Mr. Blanton's emergency need for supplemental lawyering fees; the kids who stuck around and helped out on clean-up after our successful AirJam 2K alcohol-free New Year's Eve party (I know a lot of you could have been skiing or sleeping, or gotten into champagne and narcotics because of the New Year partying and whatnot, yet you chose to be loyal to the burgeoning antidrug campaign here); and to the kids who worked closely and feverishly on our Pretzel Time/Mall of America information-gathering field trip (getting parental sig's, bidding on coaches and accommodations for me, 'cause I had the flu)—these are the kids who I want to represent themselves, me, and St. Cloud High School at this summer camp. Don't say you are too poor, because there is a scholarship-mentorship program available, and I know that you'll just be tanning by a pool anyway. Some of you I know can't go, because I've already arranged a mentorship-apprenticeship at Contempo Casuals in Fridley for you. But the rest of you, take heed:

1) Weekly camps.

2) Beautiful cabins.

3) Weekly in-kitchen and marketing reps from Wendy's, Arby's, Sbarro, Olive Garden, Shoney's, Hardee's, Hot Sam, Orange Julius, and Fannie Farmer.

4) Evenings off to swim, play Chinese checkers, other board games (no TV's) and listen to my delightful acoustic guitar work. (Think Loggins and Messina, perhaps you're too young, though.) S-MEGA teachers from Edina, Burnsville, Duluth, and Rochester will round out the staff.

5) Daily seminars with real managers and reps from The Gap, Old Navy, Coca-Cola, T.J. Maxx, and Target. We have some seasoned pros coming. They'll walk you through several different areas: displays, folding quickness, till accuracy, store upkeep, and a special VCR tape called "The Theory Behind Store Hours in Middle America."

6) Confrontation Consultation with Jim Uduro from KayBee Toys in Minneapolis. You might remember Jim from coming to class in October. He's got a great presentation on theft, embezzlement, those obnoxious customer queries that are hard to deal with, what do in case of store fire, and accidents involv-

ing blood or broken limbs or possible cardiac arrest and death of employees or customers.

7) It is in the woods. So it will be quiet and carefree. Bring mosquito repellent.

8) No parents! The camp is co-ed too!

9) Bring notebooks, pens (laptop CPUs if you have them, but don't be too showy or look down on those who don't), clean clothes, swimsuits, towels, deodorant, soap, shampoo, tooth-paste, toothbrush, and stuff like footballs or softballs and small radio/CD players. Oh, and a willingness to learn, learn, and then learn some more.

10) Plenty of quizzes, tests, and activities to sharpen your skills. Kids, this is the first time you'll say, "That was a fun quiz," or my name isn't Mr. Weeshof.

***For the rest of you complainers or non-tryers please don't bring your stinky attitudes to camp and infect the rest of us Strivers and Achievers. While the camp will be fun, it is not a place to sluff off, or try to sneak into the woods for a cig, or a canned alcoholic beverage. But even if you got a C or worse from me this year, but still want to try to make a new level for the 00–01 school year, this is the perfect opp. to do it. Level One Strivers can bump up to Level Two Strivers if they attend this camp. And Level Two Strivers probably didn't get a C or worse because they were working hard for me, but I'll be sure to bump you to a Level Three, if you come and get fulfillment out of the camp.

See me in #107.

Wallup's Theme Farm
July 18, 2000

FROM: Bob Crafft, VP Community relations
To: Employees and area media outlets
RE: Truncated camp events

Wallup's usually hosts a summer camp for children of Wallup's Workers, and has done so through early July of this year. The camp, as many of you know, is adjacent to and includes part of the Wallup's facility. In late June, following unfounded reports of impetigo and supposed eyewitness accounts of toddlers with sores that hadn't been medically addressed by professionals, and several further astonishingly unbelievable and unrealistic accounts by KXRL-TV and KRRT (1150AM), we at Wallup's deemed it best to shut down this FREE service to our employees and other area children.

Many of our employees—Cheese Criers, Art and Craft Vendors, Game Operators, Janitors, Managers, Pleasure Enhancement Providers, Cobblers, Apple Dolts, Peach Dolts, Guy-on-Wooden-Slide, Lawn Raiders, Cabineteers, Worriers, Sonnet Throwers, Bike Rental Agents, Cane, Iron Roger, Stew Servers, Xuss, Musket Infantry, Weeblers, etc.—have been and/or are currently on a furlough or prison-release program. BUT they are good people in search of chance number two. Many haven't been near their children from six months to a dozen or so years. That is many summer afternoons of not being able to peek over a snow fence and see your offspring happily playing in a haystack on a Wallup's tar lot, or attending to a baby goat, or making finger Jell-O with a supervisor who has never been arrested yet. That is many summer (and winter) afternoons of being locked up (three hots and a cot) and not working or seeing your kids up close, while they learn and go through puberty and deal with life's lessons.

This is especially sad for higher-ups at Wallup's because we feel like in closing the camp, we are lowering the boom on our

Second Chancers by saying your kids can't come to camp while you work. Just like society did, when they said "Go to Jail," to many of them without rhymes or reasons. In many ways, if we were more thin-skinned, we'd first think, "Well, how are they going to afford that?" or "This might turn them back to drug addictions or abuse, or spousal abuse. Or knocking off small gas stations to get the extra child-care money." But we have hope that our workers aren't going to fall prey to that. And they are not all ex-convicts either. There are some workers filtered in who are role models. They have kids too. These kids have mouths to feed also, and that is where that saying comes in and how you have probably heard it. "I have X-amount of mouths to feed."

Our camp kids were involved in many positive activities: we had junior Cheese Criers, and other things that encompass the Theme Farm life. We think, for example, there is no better way to learn about the value of money and dairy products than through the age-old practice of wooden-wheelbarrow-based Cheese Crying, which started in Norfolk or Philadelphia upwards of 250 years ago. We carry that through today, and some of the campers had even incorporated rap music into their cheese hawking. It was wonderful, but minus the cheese end of things, it will just be raps that probably contain swear words, because no parents will be around, because we at Wallup's refuse to be taunted or under exposé by a TV station with an ax it chooses to grind on us.

Many of these kids will now have a bridge of one month between camp and school. In the past, out of courtesy, we at Wallup's determined that any gap, or camp-to-school bridge, shouldn't be more than ten days, nor should it include more than two weekends. We are disheartened then to see this one-month bridge, because in talking to drug and graffiti specialists, we surmised that a one-month bridge is dangerous in that illegal way, and also in simpler (but costly) ways like the amount of groceries and additional electricity the kids will use at their homes by not being at camp.

Now then, were there sores?

I will address that by saying a boy, at camp, picked a knee scab on a popular day at the Theme Farm. Many visitors saw this, and one reported it to the Health Board, who we squared things away with, and then the media got involved. It was nothing more than that, and some minor impetigo cases that always occur near busy drinking fountains anyway. We always have had strong relations with the media, and even when PETA got on us about the donkey who was on the tightrope, we all worked it out, even though the donkey was a tightrope specialist (better than most humans) and always had a net beneath it.

People will know the truth, and following a few safety procedures, I ensure you the camp will be back next summer. Workers can pick up free passes to Atlas Water Park for their families, to be used on their days off at Gate H from 12–3 on Thursday, as our way of saying sorry.

Sincerely,
Bob

COMMENTS WRITTEN ON EVALUATIONS OF MY SPEECH ON NEEDLE-EXCHANGE PROGRAMS

Andy Rathbun

I like your visual aid—creative!

Great visual aid

Creative visual aid

Good job on the drawings!

I liked the visual aid it was fun and educational.

Your visual was great!

Good use of visual

Visual aid was appropriate and colorful.

Very nice visual

Visual aid assisted in keeping the audience interested.

THE NEWEST FROM JOKELAND
Brodie H. Brockie and R. J. White

BAR JOKE #1
A man walks into a bar. He has a few drinks and chats with the bartender. Later that night, he goes home alone and reflects on the poor decisions he's made in life.

RELIGIOUS JOKE #5
A priest, a minister, and a rabbi are walking down the street. They discuss, together, the various traditions and beliefs of their different religions. Each leaves with a greater respect for the others and a deeper understanding of the world.

DOCTOR JOKE #5
A man goes to his doctor. The doctor tells him he's dying.

The man says, "I want a second opinion."

The doctor gives him the name and number of a specialist in the type of cancer with which the man has been diagnosed.

POLISH JOKE #21

A gentleman is of Polish descent. His heritage is not discernible to his neighbors and co-workers, save for the letters *ski* at the end of his surname.

GENIE JOKE #3

A man and a woman are crossing the desert. They find a lamp in the sand. The man rubs the lamp and nothing happens. Afterward, he feels a bit foolish.

CHICKEN JOKE #63

Why did the chicken cross the road?

Because the chicken lacks any reasoning or decision-making capabilities, it seems unlikely that the chicken's action was spurred by any particular motivation.

DEATH JOKE #5

A man died. What transpired after he passed the veil of death is beyond the knowledge of the living.

KNOCK-KNOCK JOKE #8

Knock, knock!

Who's there?

John.

John who?

John Wilson, your old friend from college.

What a pleasant surprise. Please, come in.

BAR JOKE #17

A man walks into a bar with a dog. He orders a drink.

The bartender says, "Hey, we don't let dogs in here!"

The man says, "But I'm blind, and this is my Seeing Eye dog. According to the Americans with Disabilities Act, you have to allow him into your establishment."

The bartender gives him his drink, which he consumes.

WIFE JOKE #2
Take my wife, please, as I can no longer afford to pay for a nurse to come and care for her on a daily basis.

LAWYER JOKE #7
What do you call a room full of lawyers?
   A group of highly educated legal professionals.

BLONDE JOKE #116
How do you brainwash a blonde?
   A rigorous schedule of psychologically breaking down her confidence and resistance to outside suggestion.

FARMER'S DAUGHTER JOKE #13
A man is driving down a country road at night when his car gets a flat tire.
   He stops by a local farmhouse and asks the owner if he can stay there for the night.
   "Sure," says the farmer. "As long as you don't touch my three beautiful daughters."
   The man did as he was told because, frankly, he didn't find the girls nearly as attractive as their father seemed to.

EXCERPTS FROM MY SPEECH ON FOREST-FIRE PREVENTION

Arthur Bradford

LADIES AND GENTLEMEN, this is the time of the year that we really have to watch out. Every day now, as we sit in our homes, thousands of acres of good forest are burning to the ground ... and there is nothing we can do about it! We sometimes fly helicopters over forest fires and drop sacks of water on the flames, but that's just for show. It doesn't do any good. Even those ditches we dig and those smoke jumpers we employ have no conceivable effect on the course of a raging fire. But listen, if we put all that energy into simple PREVENTION, then we'd be a lot better off. It's a lot easier to put out a fire which has already been prevented. A LOT easier.

YOU DON'T JUST LEAVE A CAMPFIRE UNATTENDED! It could go off and destroy a national park while you weren't looking. DON'T TAKE YOUR EYES OFF THAT FIRE! Another thing which can sometimes happen is that a fire can creep along underground, unbeknownst to the firekeeper, and then it pops up fifty yards away—a forest fire. This is why I think you should always have plenty of water nearby. And don't be afraid to use it. People these days are always talking about saving water and conserving it for this and that, but what's more important, water or trees?

Well, let's look at it this way: you can make an awful lot of paper out of just a few acres of forest. And most of the animals we really love—deer, rabbits, hippos, goats—they all live in the forest. Imagine all of them burning up! Fish, for the most part, are unaffected by forest fires, which is probably why you don't hear much from water conservation activists on this subject.

I suggest we put up a fireproof barrier or something. Keep the kids out of the forests if we must. Let them play on supervised playgrounds, or indoors, at least until they can learn to handle matches properly. Also, maybe if we were to make sure things weren't so DRY out there then our hillsides might not go up in flames so easily. This gets back to my point about water conservation. We could prevent a lot of fires if we just moved a few lakes around. I understand that much of the technology which I am discussing here tonight might not actually exist, but that is no reason not to mention it.

Also, I understand that if you leave certain glass containers, like soda bottles or jars, out in the middle of a dry field, the containers can act like magnifying glasses and concentrate the sun's rays onto specific points on the ground. This, too, can start a forest fire. Someone once told me that forest fires are natural and we should let them happen. This is a lot of crap. Trees turn carbon dioxide into oxygen, which is probably the single most important gas on this planet. We probably wouldn't have any oxygen at all if it weren't for trees. I think people who believe forest fires are natural are just like people who don't use deodorant because they think the way they smell is good. No one really likes to be around such a person.

In conclusion, I'd like to make a few points about bears. Many people are afraid of bears. Small children, in particular, find them terrifying. So why, I ask you, do we employ a bear, Smokey the Bear, as our national spokesperson for forest-fire prevention? I would imagine that some children see him up there with his hat and big teeth and they think, "Let him burn." That is awful! How can we let our children feel this way? Some recent statistics have shown a startling trend toward arson-induced forest fires. That is to say, fires started by people on purpose! Damn it! What is wrong with the world today that some sick child would burn up all those trees? And bears! And frogs and foxes and all the things that call our forests home. What greater waste is there on this earth than a goddamned forest fire? When I think about all those trees out there in Idaho burning up like matchsticks just because we don't have the sense to protect them, it makes me want to puke.

Thank you for your time. Good night.

AS A PORN MOVIE TITLER, I MAY LACK PROMISE

John Moe

When Harry Met Sally, They Had Sex with One Another

The Matrix-sex

Those Magnificent Men in Their Flying Machines Are Humping

Mr. Smith Goes to Washington Whilst Having Sex

American History XXX

Reservoir Dogs Humping All Over People's Legs

All Quiet on the Western Front Except for All the People Having Sex on the Western Front

O Brother, Where Art Thou Doing It?

Sex Degrees of Sexparation

Akira Kurosawa's Dreams About Having Lots of Sex with People

You've Got Mail, and Also Tons of Sex!

It's a Wonderful Life When You Are Having Scads of Sex with Others

Some Like It Hot, e.g., Hookers

The Day the Earth Stood Still Somebody Somewhere Was Having Sex

Schindler's List of People to Have Sex with a Whole Lot

I KNOW WHAT YOU DID
TWO MOONS AGO
(THE REVENGE)

Brian Kennedy

SIGHING LAMB OPENED her large, brown, doelike eyes and stretched languorously atop her pile of furs. The morning sun filtered in through the walls of the wigwam, caressing her nubile young body with its gentle warmth. She rose to her hands and knees and peeled aside the entrance flap—and jumped back with a start as a young brave's face peered in.

"Good morning, little wood mouse," said the tall, lean warrior, his smile revealing clean, straight white teeth.

"Good morning, Wind Runner!" Sighing Lamb chirped, and yawned mightily. She raised her arms and stretched, raising her large, firm, melon-shaped breasts under her buckskin nightshirt. She stifled a giggle as she caught Wind Runner staring down at them. "Do you hunt today?"

"Yes, of course!" said Wind Runner. "Today I will catch the biggest deer you ever have seen!" He smiled again. "And bring it back, just for you," he added flirtatiously.

Sighing Lamb blushed red and blew him a kiss. "Well,

good luck, then!" Wind Runner smiled at her again and darted off to join the rest of the hunting party.

The Indian maiden sighed wistfully as she watched the Squab braves prancing off to the hunting grounds, their tight buckskin breeches flapping in the spring wind. Why couldn't she go too? she thought to herself. She wanted to bathe in the blood of Brother Deer, to bring home provisions for her tribespeople. But no! She was a woman, and destined to a life of mending buckskin breeches, digging in the dirt for roots and tubers, nursing babies at her teats. Why couldn't things be different?

"We come together to celebrate the opening of our new Burial Ground," said Chief Falling Owl, speaking stiffly from behind a podium hewn from a great tree stump. "May this land help our people find their way to the Spirit World; may it be forever free from the Wendigo's predations, from the Water Monster's rages. May it find favor with the Manidog and the Wenebojo, and may they deem it worthy of their protection.

"And now let us feast!" said Chief Falling Owl beatifically. The Squab uttered a ragged cheer and descended upon the long tables groaning with venison, roots, tubers, berries, and other victuals.

Unseen in the bushes, something watched them.

"This is a horrible thing," Grizzled Fist said, squatting on his haunches and staring at the two corpses. They had been killed while making love—a single primitive flint spear transfixed the naked bodies, pinning them to the bearskin bed and thence to the floor of the wigwam. "Yes, it is horrible," Grizzled Fist continued. As assistant war chief, it was his job to investigate such occurrences, but he had never before seen something like this.

"I also think that it is horrible," said his rookie partner, With-Great-Hair. "Who would do such a thing?"

"I do not know," snarled Grizzled Fist. "But we must not rest until we find him. And give him a taste of his own medicine." Grizzled Fist had a reputation as a "loose arrow" among the warriors of the Squab; he was a man who preferred actions to words, who had no patience for the inconvenience and tedium of tribal regulations.

"You mean 'arrest him and bring him to justice,' Grizzled Fist." With-Great-Hair was more inclined to play by the rules; the two made an excellent team, With-Great-Hair's cautious nature proving the perfect foil to Grizzled Fist's reckless tendencies.

Grizzled Fist merely snarled and stared out the door of the wigwam. With-Great-Hair wrapped a piece of rawhide around his hand and carefully removed the spear. The roughly hewn flint spearhead fell off. With-Great-Hair gently picked it up with two sticks and placed it in a hemp bag for later identification.

"Did you hear?" said Lips-Like-Sugar at the ceremonial dinner that night. Her father was Chief Falling Owl; he had given her a beautiful white horse and lavished upon her many glass beads and other expensive baubles. This made her the most popular of the daughters of the wealthy tribesmen; she ruled the other Squab girls with an iron fist, and brooked no dissension. "They found Little Dove and Prancing Cricket," she said, and then her voice dropped to a conspiratorial whisper. "Dead! And guess what they were doing?"

"What a slut," cackled Lips-Like-Sugar's friend, Climbs-Over-Boulders, nibbling daintily on a piece of dried venison. "And with Prancing Cricket! When was the last time he slew a buffalo for the tribe's provisions! Do you remember last hunting season, when he ran in terror from the stampeding herd?"

Sighing Lamb looked up from her meal in shock. "Why do

you say these things?" she asked, amazed. "They were fellow tribespeople, and now they are dead!" Tears began to flow from her beautiful brown eyes. "How could you be so cruel?"

Lips-Like-Sugar turned toward her, scorn in her eyes. "Why, you seem very interested in this," she said. "Very interested. Perhaps you had feelings deep in your Inner Heart for Prancing Cricket yourself?"

The other girls cackled with delight; Sighing Lamb's cheeks burned. She stood up from the communal fire and took her earthenware bowl to the washing place. What was happening to these people? she thought to herself, and her eyes filled with tears. What was happening to them all?

Skritch. Skritch. There was something at the flap of the wigwam. Grizzled Fist jerked upright from his pile of furs and grabbed for his tomahawk. Stay calm, he told himself, and remember to slash at the throat. He jerked the flap aside and raised his tomahawk. "AIAIAIAAAA!!!" he cried, and raised his arm to strike.

With-Great-Hair fell face-first through the opening, a primitive stone spear protruding from his back. "My back," he moaned. "There is a primitive stone spear in it. I fear I am dying."

"Do not worry! It will be all right," said Grizzled Fist. He bit his lip in anger—truthfully, he knew that there was nothing he could do. With-Great-Hair would be dead soon.

"I do not know who did this," said With-Great-Hair, his teeth clenched in agony. "A dark, shadowy figure, dressed in untanned skins, with strange hair and clothing … agh!" And then he died.

"Rest in peace, brave With-Great-Hair," said Grizzled Fist, and gently closed his dead partner's eyes. And may I avenge you and put an end to this horror, he thought to himself.

*　　*　　*

Lips-Like-Sugar sprinted through the forest, her mind numb with terror, branches whipping her face and tearing at her hair. She could hear footsteps behind her, and a dry, husklike, rattling breathing.

Why had she gone with Sings-With-Trees to the Burial Ground? She cursed her stupidity, and her attraction to the Indian lacrosse athlete-warrior. She should have known there was something wrong with that place. Now Sings-With-Trees lay still in a pile of broken limbs, joining the other corpses in the graveyard—and Lips-Like-Sugar was running for her life.

The Indian maid tripped on a branch and fell to the ground, skinning her knees and elbows. She wiped blood from her mouth and staggered to her feet, and began running again. The breathing behind her was closer.

You can beat this! Lips-Like-Sugar's mind screamed. She was the Squab's fastest woman sprinter; she ran miles every day to maintain her slender figure and to one day attract a husband of high status who would maintain her in the manner to which she was accustomed. Her expensive beaded moccasins pounded at the soil as she ran faster and faster. The ghoulish breathing behind her slowly grew fainter as Lips-Like-Sugar gathered speed. "Just try to catch me, Wendigo!" she yelled in triumph.

She rounded a bend in the trail, and suddenly the forest gave way to scattered shrubbery. She was standing at the top of a gently sloping hill—and at the bottom lay her village, the wigwams bathed in moonlight. She'd made it!

Lips-Like-Sugar uttered an exhausted whoop! of glee and staggered down the hillside toward home. She suddenly felt something strike her back with incredible force, and stared numbly at a bloody spear point protruding through her fine beaded buckskin tunic. She had not made it after all.

The shadowy figure folded her into its arms and disappeared into the darkness. Lips-Like-Sugar's dying shriek echoed through the forest, and then the woods were silent again.

"Yes, Granddaughter?" the wizened shaman said from behind the half-opened wigwam door. His head peeked through the door; huge dark circles limned his eyes, lines of worry furrowed his brow. He looked as if he had not slept for several days.

Sighing Lamb hid her shock and composed herself. "Grandfather, I am here to ask you a question. These recent murders that have plagued our tribe—are they somehow connected with the recent construction of our Burial Ground? All of these horrible things started happening when our tribe built it."

The shaman sighed. "Come in," he said. Once they were inside his cluttered wigwam, the shaman continued. "You are wise beyond your years, Granddaughter. I fear you are right; I have spent the evening consulting the Manidog, and what they have to tell us is terrible and sad. We have built our Indian burial ground ..."

"Yes!? What?!" Sighing Lamb snapped impatiently.

"On top of an ancient Indian burial ground!" the shaman wailed piteously.

Sighing Lamb gasped and clutched her hands to her chest. Outside, a wolf howled. Aaarrrrrooooooooooooooo.

When a member of the Squab was laid to rest, his body was washed and dressed in his finest clothing, his hair was braided, and he was taken up in several sheets of birch bark. His favorite valuables—knives, spears, tobacco, jewelry, and the like—were buried with him.

Also buried with him were a spoon, a kettle, and a dish—all of them essential for the four-day journey that the soul of the Squab had to take before it reached its final resting place. On the first day, the soul had to confront a shaking log lying across a stream; he would be able to pass by addressing the log as "Grandfather," and scattering tobacco in the stream as tribute. Afterward, he would meet his escort to Heaven, Chia'bos, the younger brother of the legendary warrior Wi'ske. Each evening the soul would stop, build a fire, and prepare a meal for himself and Chia'bos, and each evening his surviving relatives would build a fire around his grave in support. At the end of the fourth day, his hair was braided, and Chia'bos and the soul would enter heaven—and the relatives would throw a great feast in celebration of his successful journey.

The victims of the eldritch horror that plagued the Squab had not yet been given this honor. The tribal shaman had judged it unwise to inter them until their inhuman murderer had been defeated, lest it follow them into the afterlife and destroy their souls as well as their bodies.

Sighing Lamb reflected carefully on all this as she gazed upon the Burial Ground of the Squab. "I am sorry, eldritch horror!" she called to the bodies, her voice quavering. "We did not mean to build our Indian burial ground on top of yours! What can we do to make amends?"

"RAAAARRRRRRRRR!!!!!!" howled a shadowy, shaggy figure as it advanced from the bushes toward her.

Sighing Lamb sobbed in terror and fell to the ground. "I am sorry we did this…. I am sorry. Please do not kill me."

The primitive figure raised his spear and snarled with glee—and uttered a gurgling cry of pain, staggering backward and dropping his spear. "Leave her alone!" Grizzled Fist bellowed, a bloody tomahawk gripped firmly in a white-knuckled hand.

"RARRRRRR!!!!" uttered the ancient Indian, and tackled the burly Indian detective. The two rolled about in the charnel earth of the burial ground. Sighing Lamb shrieked and hid behind a large rock, her eyes squeezed shut and her hands pressed over her ears.

The battle was long and bloody, but Grizzled Fist finally gained the upper hand. He pinned the writhing ancient Indian to the ground and raised his tomahawk. "This is for With-Great-Hair!" he snarled—the tomahawk came down one, two, three times, and the ancient Indian lay still in a bloody heap on the ground.

Sighing Lamb leaned back wearily against the nearest tree. This was all just too much! Grizzled Fist staggered forward, equally exhausted, and the two embraced. "Don't worry, little one. It is over now," he said. "It is over. The Wendigo, or whatever it was, has been laid to rest."

"No," said Sighing Lamb softly. "It was no Wendigo." They turned to the rapidly stiffening corpse. "Just the ghost of one who came before. We must help him rest now.

"We must abandon this place and shun it forever more," she continued. "For this is not our land. We Indians do not know how to preserve the earth, only destroy it. We need to learn from those who came before us, lest we follow them into oblivion."

Grizzled Fist smiled softly. "I think you have given us all something to think about. May I take you out for venison, tubers, and berries some time?"

"Yes, I would like that," Sighing Lamb said, and smiled tiredly. Perhaps something good would come of this after all.

WORDS THAT WOULD MAKE NICE NAMES FOR BABIES, IF IT WEREN'T FOR THEIR UNSUITABLE MEANINGS

Stephany Aulenback

FOR GIRLS

Angina
Calorie
Dyslexia
Feta
Plaice
Reciprocity
Uvula

FOR BOYS

Bench
Caftan
Chyle
Raunch
Rennet
Roily
Torrid
Thwart
Fellatio

REVIEWS OF MY DAYDREAMS
T. G. Gibbon

TITLE: "Hail to President Tom"

WHEN: Without fail, I have gotten this daydream while watching *20/20* or *60 Minutes* any time in the last thirteen years.

SYNOPSIS: With epic scope, this forty-three-second fantasy follows me through several grueling political campaigns and concludes with my years as a widely admired and distinguished elder statesman. Retirement suits me, I have to say, and my accomplishments while in office were great and lasting, such as nationalizing industry and education, eliminating poverty, and formulating a powerful foreign policy, all with my winning, if disturbingly flip, personal style. Plus I enjoy JFK-like adoration from female citizens.

EVALUATION: A common premise for the politically aware delusions-of-grandeur set but somewhat redeemed by my noapologies leftist ways and wickedly snide comments at debates. (America laughed as I destroyed dedicated fascists with just a few well-placed bons mots.) All in all, however, a bit pompous. Do I really expect myself to believe a president with holes in the elbows of his jackets? Do women have to like me in all my daydreams? Grow up, Tom!

*   *   *

TITLE: "Tom Under Fire"

WHEN: At home, watching the television, when I get up to go to the bathroom or kitchen.

SYNOPSIS: I'm back in World War I and right in the thick of all that fighting that was so popular then. I run through an elaborate trench system in Flanders. I think it's Flanders. Looks like Flanders. Could be Picardy. Ends with me getting shot in the face just when my side is on the cusp of victory.

EVALUATION: The mournful tone that springs from its subterranean milieu is punctuated and brought to a transcendent conclusion by the narrator's death, which hovers between suicide and heroism, in what is at best an ethical gray area. Still, a touching and exciting romp. A boy's adventure fantasy by way of Sartre, with a touch of martyrdom for spice and tears.

*   *   *

TITLE: "Welcome Back, Tom"

WHEN: On the bus. Payday.

SYNOPSIS: At some point I go to graduate school and return to my high school to teach history. In the classroom I deliver enchanting lectures, each predicated on the importance of memorizing names and dates. They eat it up, the students. Later, in my capacity as the most popular dormitory master ever, I lounge around turning the kids on to "free-thinking." The boys are enchanted by my beautiful wife, and the girls are more than mildly intrigued by my jet-setting lifestyle and effortless self-confidence. Soul-searching third act has me wondering whether to send my son to this school. Will it be too awkward for him to be under his father's considerable shadow?

EVALUATION: A pastoral piece with enough *Goodbye, Mr. Chips* to carry it along for a while. But several important questions are left unanswered: Will institutional life make me conservative? And what happens when my wife and I get old and less attractive to the kids? Will my charisma diminish? Will they even want me as a dormitory master? Satisfying on the surface, but does not hold up under scrutiny. Isn't it just a death-in-life-meets-perpetual-adolescence scenario? Also bears uncomfortable similarities to the "distinguished former statesman" sequence of the above presidential fantasy.

*   *   *

NEXT TIME: Reviews of "Tom's Suicide" and "Tom, the Celebrity of Some Renown."

INSOMNIACS! I BRING WORDS OF HOPE AND WISDOM

Jason Roeder

GREETINGS, SLEEPLESS!

I just wanted to let you know how revitalized I'm feeling after yet another successful night's rest. Didn't quite grab eight hours if you deduct my trip to the bathroom and my having to reposition the cat that one time, but in each case you'll be pleased to hear that I was able to resume my sleep almost immediately. (My dreams spliced together seamlessly, I might add.) There's nothing extraordinary about what I did, of course—any normal person could pull it off—but boy, did it feel good!

Now, I want to help you, if you'll let me. My first recommendation is that you turn the clock toward the wall. This way, you can end the torment of those molten numbers hovering in the darkness as you fail to sleep. It's absolutely critical, however, that you not stay awake wondering if your mental tally of elapsed hours and minutes matches that of the clock's display. I bet you could exhaust a whole night doing that.

You also might want to consider visualization. Come up

with a mental task intended to draw your attention away from the effort of nodding off, thereby allowing your automatic sleep mechanisms to engage. You can imagine something dull, like a sequence of numbers, or project yourself into a more engrossing scenario: "I am the Super Bowl MVP"; "I am Malcolm X"; "I am the Hamburglar." Of course you'll need to be wary of the fact that the gnawing, self-conscious awareness of visualizing can get in the way of actually engaging in said visualization.

But maybe you don't even need my advice. Perhaps you can use the late hours to work on your novel, your quilt, or your Battle of Shiloh diorama—anything to distract you from the fact that recent studies showed that people who went without sleep for nineteen hours scored significantly lower on reflex tests than people with a blood-alcohol level of .08. (That's the legal standard for intoxication in many states.) And whether you've just poured calamine lotion in your cereal or stitched up Mr. Clark after his cesarean section, I implore you not to dwell on the reams of research attesting to how sleep deprivation impairs memory and judgment and is even correlated to a significantly shortened life span. Likewise, while you're waiting outside an elementary school for a random kindergarten teacher to pistol-whip, keep in mind that a good night's sleep, which you're incapable of, dramatically improves mood. I should stop here. You probably want to jump into a shower that you won't be able to feel against your insensate zombie flesh and get out into a world of people and objects that will all seem fatally distant and unreal.

Besides, I have a productive day ahead of me.

THE TEN WORST FILMS OF ALL TIME, AS REVIEWED BY EZRA POUND OVER ITALIAN RADIO

Greg Purcell

Bambi
Filth.

Casablanca
This movie is filth.

Cat People
A race may civilize itself *by language,* not film. *Cat People* is filth.

Gentleman Jim
To the Animals who made this usurious film: god damn you.

The Magnificent Ambersons
This movie is indistinguishable from the filth-rustlings of swine in a sty.

The Man Who Came to Dinner
May you choke on it, bacilli.

Yankee Doodle Dandy
I sort of liked James Cagney's filthy Irish energy in this one.

The Palm Beach Story
Bless: The Italian *Dolcestilnovisti,* the "sweet new style" current in the time of the papish Guelphs and the imperial Ghibellines. One will particularly take heed of its foremost practitioner, Guido Cavalcanti.

Blast: Preston Sturges and the Jewish moneylenders who helped him to make this film.

Now, Voyager
Two boils for the director's infected liver.

This Gun for Hire
This film reeks of syphilis. Filth.

GROUP MOBILIZATION AS A DESPERATE CRY FOR HELP

Christopher Monks

HELLO!

You are invited to take part in a flash mob, the project that creates an inexplicable mob of people for ten minutes or less, in the front yard of my ex-girlfriend Deborah's house, tomorrow at 6:13 p.m. Please tell anybody else who you think might be interested in joining us.

INSTRUCTIONS:

1. We'll meet outside the Crazy Pizza around the corner from Deborah's place. Be there by 6 p.m. Please be respectful of Crazy Pizza's employees and patrons, and refrain from ordering pizza or Crazy Cinnaballs.

2. At exactly 6:05 p.m. I will pass out slips of paper with general instructions and poster boards. One-third of the poster boards will read "I will never stop lovin' you, Deborah"; one-third will read "Why do you insist on ruining my life?"; and

one-third will read "Please don't throw out my comic book collection."

3. Once the instructions and poster boards have been passed out, I will organize the group. All of the guys who are better looking than me will be sent to the back and will be required to wear sad clown masks. If I find that a better-looking-than-me guy in a sad clown mask is still better-looking than me I will ask him to leave. This may seem a little paranoid, but you don't know Deborah like I know Deborah. All of the just-as-good-looking-as-me guys will be placed in the middle of the line, and the guys who I think are uglier than me will get to be in the front. Women can choose to be wherever they want.

4. At 6:10 p.m. we will walk over in a silent and orderly fashion to Deborah's place. Really hot-looking women are encouraged to walk with me, hold my hand, and act like I'm their new boyfriend.

5. We will arrive at Deborah's at 6:13 p.m. sharp. Please arrange yourself in Deborah's front yard in the same order you were in while walking over. Depending on the size of the mob, some of the better-looking-than-me guys in sad clown masks may have to stand on the sidewalk. Please don't complain about it if this is necessary. Be tough.

6. Once we are organized in our appropriate places, everyone should take a moment to notice the rhododendron bush in Deborah's yard. I bought that for her in celebration of our three-month anniversary. I planted it for her, too. While the bush won't be in bloom, please believe me when I tell you that its flowers are only eclipsed in beauty by Deborah's magnificent emerald green eyes.

7. We will then stand quietly in Deborah's front yard for five minutes or until Deborah comes out of her house. If any

bystander should happen by and ask you what is going on, politely answer, "I'm a fan of doughnuts, and this is the home of the Doughnut Queen."

8. If after five minutes Deborah hasn't come out of her house, I will ring her doorbell. As soon as Deborah opens her door, those people with the "I will never stop lovin' you, Deborah" posters should stoically raise them above their heads. Everybody else will begin singing the Peter Gabriel song "In Your Eyes." Be sure to really sell the tune. No mumbling.

9. My bet is that Deborah will be embarrassed at first. She'll blush and smile and not know what to say. At 6:19 lower the signs and stop singing. It's then when I'll ask her to take me back. However, I'm sure that Deborah, being Deborah, will break my heart yet again. When she does, those holding the "Why do you insist on ruining my life?" posters will raise them up. Everyone else will then sing "Love Bites" by Def Leppard. If you want to try to hum the guitar solo part feel free.

10. This will no doubt make Deborah upset, and her ugly side will soon be on display for all to see. Don't be afraid; just stand your ground and continue singing. She'll probably say means things like, "He still owes me $927.00 for back rent," or "He tried to French kiss my sister," but pay her no mind. I'm not even attracted to her sister. Honest.

11. Any better-looking-than-me guy in a sad clown mask that tries to take advantage of the situation by offering to console Deborah will be asked to leave.

12. As Deborah's calling the police, those holding the "Please don't throw out my comic book collection" posters will raise them up. Everybody else will sing "If You're Happy and You Know It Clap Your Hands."

13. At 6:23 p.m. or when we hear the sirens, whichever comes first, we will disperse in an orderly manner. I may stick around for a bit, but don't bother waiting for me; I'll be curled up and crying by the rhododendron bush. I feel it is something I just need to do. So go on. I'll be all right.

Thanks! I look forward to seeing you tomorrow. It'll be great. Things are really starting to look up for me. I can feel it. In the slight chance Deborah is not home when we get to her front yard we will return to Crazy Pizza, get something to eat, and try again later.

FIRE: THE NEXT SHARP STICK?
John Hodgman

The offices of Ten Men Who Help Each Other But Are Not Brothers, a firm located Near the River That's Not as Wide as the Really Wide River.

[ONE WHO HELPS THE HAIRY ONE is seated, going over some notes. Enter MAKER OF FIRE.]

ONE [*standing*]: Hey, it's good to see you. Thanks for coming by.

MAKER: Thank you, One Who Helps the Hairy One. I'm sorry I'm late. Somehow I ended up by the Really Wide River.

ONE: Really? When we met by the Sticky Tree, I thought I said Near the River That's Not as Wide as the Really Wide River.

MAKER: That is what you said. I must have gotten turned around at the Sharp Shells.

ONE: Oh, yeah. That happens a lot.

MAKER: I must have just spaced.

ONE: No harm done. Do you want a Stick That Tastes Good to gnaw on?

MAKER: No thanks. I just had one. I'm a bear if I don't have one before Hot Part of the Day.

ONE [*doesn't understand, a little afraid*]: Excuse me?

MAKER [*laughs*]: Sorry. Sorry. I'm not *actually* a bear. I just mean that I'm *like* a bear if I don't have a Stick That Tastes Good.

ONE: You pretend to be a bear?

MAKER: No. I feel like a bear feels when he wakes up. You know, grumpy, impatient.

ONE: Do you become a bear when you say it?

MAKER: No. I just say it.

ONE [*still doesn't understand*]: Oh. Okay. I see. Well, in a way, that's exactly why I asked you to come down here. As you know, Ten Men Who Help Each Other But Are Not Brothers is a very old and established firm.

MAKER: I do know.

ONE: I mean, for me, it's a real honor to be associated with the Hairy One and to be his Helper. The Hairy One's a visionary, you know. But he's, how do I say it? He's older than the Old One, and as a result, I think that Ten Men needs to think about its future and think about how it can stay competitive in changing times.

MAKER: Naturally, I agree.

ONE: When we met by the Sticky Tree, I immediately thought, here's a guy who's ahead of the curve. Here's a guy who maybe can help Ten Men make the transition into That Day Which Isn't This Day, But Also Isn't the Day Before or the Day Before.

MAKER: At the Shallow Pond with a Terrible Odor, we call it "Tomorrow."

ONE: Really? "Tomorrow"? Very clever. But the point is, we were talking about fire. And it seemed to me after we spoke that this could be just the thing to carry Ten Men into "Tomorrow."

MAKER: Well, there's no question that fire has a lot to offer any firm, Ten Men included, and I'm happy to show you why. But I think you need to think seriously about what your fire needs are. The truth is, this technology is so revolutionary that I think the real question won't be whether fire is right for Ten Men, but whether Ten Men is ready for fire.

ONE [*nodding seriously*]: True. True. Well, what I have planned is pretty informal, just a meeting of the minds, so to speak. I've asked the Hairy One to sit in on this meeting, since he'll have to approve anything that might happen Not Now, But Another Time. You may have to take it a little slow with him— he's a bit of a Neanderthal when it comes to this sort of thing, if you know what I mean.

MAKER: HA HA HA HA HA HA!

ONE: HA HA HA HA HA HA!

[*Enter the HAIRY ONE, carrying a sharp stick. One immediately stops laughing and falls to the floor completely prostrate, arms and legs spread, face down. MAKER smirks and does not move.*]

ONE [*speaking into the floor*]: Oh, hey, Hairy One, how are you? Thanks for coming by.

HAIRY ONE [*Grunts. To MAKER*]: Where are the Sticks That Taste Good?

MAKER: I think they're over there.

[*HAIRY ONE crosses to side table to get a stick and begins gnawing it.*]

ONE [*starting to raise himself*]: I just gathered them, Hairy One, so they're fresh. [*Pauses. Looks to MAKER*] You know me: I'm a bear if I don't have one before the Time You Tell Us When We Can Eat.

HAIRY ONE [*stick drops from mouth in fear*]: Bear! Bear!

[*Raises sharp stick and crosses to begin hitting ONE with it.*]

ONE: No! Not bear! Not bear!

MAKER: It's just a saying.

ONE: It's just a saying!

[*HAIRY ONE stops his attack and stares at both of them suspiciously.*]

ONE [*rising, then sitting down*]: I'm not a bear.

MAKER: It's just something that he said.

HAIRY ONE [*completely uninterested*]: Whatever. [*Retrieves stick and sits down at head of table.*]

ONE: Hairy One, Maker of Fire. Maker of Fire, the Hairy One.

MAKER: My pleasure, Hairy One. I've followed your work with Ten Men for a long time. It's a remarkable firm.

HAIRY ONE: So you're the one with the fire?

MAKER: Yes.

HAIRY ONE: Is it here?

MAKER: Well, no.

HAIRY ONE: Where is it?

MAKER: Well, in a sense, Hairy One, fire is everywhere. Rather than being an object, like, say, your sharp stick, it's really a process, and so it can't really be said to exist anywhere. In a sense, fire exists in its own imaginary, virtual space, where we can only talk about what is not fire, and what might become fire.

HAIRY ONE: Whoa, whoa, whoa! English, please!

ONE: I think that what the Maker of Fire is trying to say is that—and let me know if I have it right—while I may have one fire, and you may have another fire in another place, and the One Who Helps the Hairy One may be planning to make a fire, the truth is that it's all fire. It's all the same thing. It's all fire.

MAKER: That's true, in a rudimentary sense, but for our purposes, it'll do fine.

ONE: What's great about fire, Hairy One, is that it combines many things in one. Light, heat, pain—all in one. It's all those things. It's a multi-thing.

HAIRY ONE: I thought you said it was all the same thing.

ONE: It is!

HAIRY ONE: But now you say it's a multi-thing?

[*ONE is confused; looks to MAKER OF FIRE.*]

MAKER: It is and it isn't. It depends on how you define "thing."

HAIRY ONE: And where does the bear come in?

MAKER: It doesn't.

ONE: That was just something I said.

HAIRY ONE: I get that, OK? I just wanted to know if a bear was involved in fire or not.

MAKER: It isn't.

HAIRY ONE: Good.

MAKER: See, the thing about fire is that it's totally interactive. Fire isn't a bear, but if you put fire on a bear, then the bear becomes fire. It's completely responsive to your needs at a given time, reacting specifically to your fuel input and usage paradigm....

HAIRY ONE: OK, stop right there. Here's the thing. I've heard a lot about this fire already. Everyone is saying how shiny it is and how flickery it is. But you have to agree that that's very specialized. I know you folks at the Shallow Pond with a Terrible Odor are making a whole big deal about this, but we here by the River That's Not as Wide as the Really Wide River, well, we're simple folk. We want to know: What can it do for us? And the thing is, until people really figure out how fire can be used, I just can't see it becoming a staple of everyday life.

ONE: If I can just jump in here for a moment, Hairy One, think of it like the sharp stick. You know, Many Many Many Nights ago, everyone was using a blunt stick for clubbing and for poking at things we had no name for. We didn't even call it blunt stick back then. We just called it stick.

MAKER: Exactly.

ONE: And then someone came along and said, hey, let's take this rock and push it on the stick and remove parts of the stick at one end until it's different than it was before. Everyone called this one Crazy One, until Crazy One took the sharp stick and put it in the Loud One's eye.

HAIRY ONE: Crazy One didn't do that. *I* did.

ONE: That's what I'm saying. Once we had the sharp stick, the Loud One became One Eye, and the Crazy One became the Big Hairy One.

HAIRY ONE: *I'm* the Big Hairy One.

ONE: That's what I'm saying. You don't want to be the One Who Didn't Like Fire. Fire is the Sharp Stick of … of … Tomorrow.

HAIRY ONE: What's Tomorrow?

MAKER: Well, that's not entirely a correct analogy, since fire can't really be compared to anything that isn't fire, but ...

HAIRY ONE [*to ONE*]: OK, but I think you're both overlooking an important thing: Fire is very very scary. Even when sharp stick got big, there were a lot of people still using blunt stick because they knew what blunt stick could do. People still love their blunt sticks, and it is many many days and nights later. So I can't see how this fire thing is going to work until people have a reason not to be scared.

MAKER: Well, before we go on, we have to all accept that not everything is going to appeal to Johnny Blunt Stick.

HAIRY ONE: OK, but let me tell you that it's Johnny Blunt Sticks that made Ten Men one of the top firms by the River That's Not as Wide as the Really Wide River. Johnny Blunt Sticks like me.

MAKER: Look, I didn't mean to offend anyone. Listen, I have to use the dungheap. Why don't I step out for a moment, and you two can decide how you want this meeting to go. OK?

HAIRY ONE: No offense, no offense. We'll be here.

[*MAKER exits.*]

ONE: I'm sure he didn't mean to suggest that ...

HAIRY ONE: I don't care about that. I know how they are by the Shallow Pond. You know I've met him before?

ONE: You have?

HAIRY ONE: Sure. Many many many many nights ago on a business trip. I was over by the Shallow Pond, and all the Shallow Ponders were laughing at him. You know what they used to call him? I mean, before all this "Maker of Fire" bullshit?

ONE: What?

HAIRY ONE: They used to call him the One Who Knocks Two Rocks Together Over Dry, Dead Plants.

ONE: Oh, man, really?

HAIRY ONE: He's a complete lunatic. Not just Not Like Us—not like anybody.

ONE: But what about fire?

HAIRY ONE: Oh, he may have fire, but "Maker of Fire"? He's an idiot. Where did you meet him?

ONE: Over by the Sticky Tree. He wanted to know if Ten Men would want to give him some food and then he would give us some fire.

HAIRY ONE: He what?!

ONE: He called it "barter."

HAIRY ONE: Well, I call it bullshit. He's obviously deranged. I thought he was here to invite us to go to the Shallow Pond and kill everyone and take fire.

ONE: No, he wants to "trade."

HAIRY ONE: Now I just feel sorry for him.

[*Reenter MAKER OF FIRE*]

MAKER: Well, have you thought it over?

HAIRY ONE: Maker of Fire, you do us great honor by traveling so far to visit we Two Men of the Ten Men Who Help Each Other But Are Not Brothers. But until I get a sense of how fire could ever be useful, I'm afraid we're just going to have to muddle along without it.

MAKER: I understand. Not all are fire-ready.

HAIRY ONE: And I'm sorry about the Johnny Blunt Stick business. Please, come over here and join hands.

[*MAKER goes to join hands. THE HAIRY ONE stabs him with the stick, and then beats him until he is dead.*]

ONE: What are you doing?

HAIRY ONE: There, he's out of his misery, poor fellow. Now go through his skins and his magic bag.

ONE: What? Why?

HAIRY ONE: We're looking for fire, my Helper! We're looking for fire!

ONE: Oh, you truly are the Wise and Big Hairy One!

FINIS

NOT VERY SCARY MOVIES

Joshua Watson

The Island of Dr. Huxtable
The Furry
The Sixth Sheikh's Sixth Sense
The Howlin'
Cat Person
I Was a Thirtysomething Werewolf
Invasion of the Body Stockings
The Thang
Friday the 11th
Something Wicked May Come by Here

CANDLE PARTY

Alysia Gray Painter

I'D LIKE TO welcome you here tonight. Everyone comfy?

Who brought a guest? I see new people here, fresh faces. Greetings, future friends! I've got some terrif news for you. Guests get a free candle, our Lodenberry Meadows tea light. This is our newest flavor, but when I say flavor I mean smell. I just call them flavors because they're nearly scrumptious enough to eat. I like the name Lodenberry. If I write that book I've been talking about, I'll call the castle in it Lodenberry Manor and the duke Lord Loden, or Lod for short, or Loddie when the main character, Drusilla or Dru for short, is being flirty. I've told you girls about my book, right? It has some wisecracking ghosts in it and an invisible gondola but I won't utter another peep about it. You'll just have to wait until it's on the bestseller list.

Now, I think we all have something in common. I'm talking about our fascination for candles. I want to see a show of hands here, who loves candles? Let me do a count. One, two, three, seven, eight, twelve. Well, it's official, everyone loves 'em.

And if you're lying I'll hold the truth candle to you and it'll burn you. Not really. Only joshing.

Bet you don't know the history of candles. Whoever can tell me the year the candle came to be gets a free Sinnamon Kiss 3.2-ounce jar. That's cinnamon with an "S," girls, and I'll leave the rest up to your filthy minds. Anyone? Karen? What'd you say? 1978? Who knew we had a comedian among us? Here's one for you, Karen. How many women does it take to light a candle? None, because no one can hold a candle to a great woman. I might use that in my book.

Okay, girls, give up? 12,339 B.C., give or take a B.C. The usage of candles predates the invention of the wheel. In fact, when those ol' cavewomen wanted their husbands to put down the club after a hard day hunting woolly elephants, those Cro-Magnon cuties shaped some animal fat into a charming votive and lit it right there under the stalactites.

Who can name what the first wicks were made out of? There's a ten-inch Lemon Drop pillar in it for you. Who wants this Lemon Drop pillar, which will burn for five to eight hours under close supervision? Do I have to keep this Lemon Drop pillar for myself? Anyone? Okay, the first wicks were made out of human hair. It's true! Who wants to volunteer some of her own luscious locks for a demonstration? Oh, come on girls, someone's got hair to spare. Nobody? I'm just pulling your wicks.

On the coffee table you'll see several of our various sizes and colors. Our biggest seller has to be this Sunshine Sunflower, which if you'll notice has a sun where the flower should be, only with petals. The sun is so versatile, really, when you think about it. You can draw a smile on it and it is happy, or make it look like a flower. And a candle with a sun on it is much nicer then the real sun, because a candle warms you gently rather than instantly incinerating you. It's all in my book.

What's my favorite candle? You always ask the toughies, don't you, Pam? I'd have to say Brownie Bliss makes my toes curl. If I met my soul mate tomorrow and he didn't like the smell of Brownie Bliss, I'd give him the old heave-ho. No cookie, no nookie, am I right, girls?

On that note, anyone here seen my soul mate? I can't seem to find him. You too, hon? I find candles to be a wonderful substitute for a love life. They make a lonely apartment passionate, only passionate without someone to talk with you and hold you. When this Leaftown Breeze pillar burns evenly for between five and eight hours and fills the room with a springtime aroma, it really can make you feel like you might be in love, only not really. I'll give this Magical Mint votive to anyone here who hates love. No one? We must all love love, right?

So here are the order forms. Just fill out your info and all that. If you'd ever like to be a Wax Witch like me and host one of these blowouts, I'll be glad to gab with you after the party. These bashes are such a giggle, you meet people and get a supply of candles to last throughout the year. It's a fun life, wicks and schticks. No, hon, schticks, not sticks. Like my schtick, me making jokes up here. Just fill out your form. Right, concentrate.

Oh, almost forgot, I've got an Apricottage Dream votive for anyone who can tell me which famous actress travels with her own personal candle-maker. Very famous. Own candle-maker. Makes candles for this star. Big celebrity. Apricottage Dream. Anyone?

IT'S NOT ACTUALLY
A SMALL WORLD

Tom Ruprecht

LAST WEDNESDAY Alden Provost was in the United terminal at O'Hare. At the same time Justin Stangel, Alden's childhood friend, was in the Continental terminal. The two grew up next door to each other, but hadn't seen one another since Justin's family moved away twenty years before. One hundred eighty thousand people pass through O'Hare every day, and the United and Continental terminals are located quite a ways away from each other, so Alden and Justin didn't even come close to bumping into each other.

Don Mackinnon was walking to work when he thought he spotted Mrs. Zelikson, his fourth-grade teacher, up ahead. Don raced after the woman and stopped her. It turned out not to be Mrs. Zelikson; in fact, this woman didn't even speak English.

Billy Norrett met Nancy Agostini at a party in Boston. During the conversation, Billy mentioned he had gone to

Duke. Nancy told him she knew tons of people who went to Duke and proceeded to rattle off four or five names. They were all a few years ahead of Billy, and he didn't know any of them.

After undergoing a religious awakening, Rich Killeen quit his job as an investment banker and became an English teacher in a small village outside Calcutta. Some afternoons he sat and watched the village women gather water from the Ganges. As he sat basking in the late-day sun, Rich occasionally thought about how remarkable it would be if he suddenly spotted someone he knew from his old life in New York strolling by the river. He never did.

A few years ago all the living presidents met for a dedication at the Reagan Library. Jimmy Carter was getting a glass of lemonade prior to the ceremony when Gerald Ford spotted him across the room. Ford ran over and exclaimed, "Oh my God, Jimmy! Imagine running into you here of all places! What are the odds?" When Ford left, Carter turned to his wife and muttered, "What a tool."

While driving around Ireland's west coast, Jay Johnson's car broke down in Dingle. Waiting for it to be fixed at the local garage, Jay stopped into a tiny pub—Tir Na Nog. There, four thousand miles from home, in a small pub with a thatched roof and six people speaking Gaelic, Jay didn't know a damn person.

Jean Chappelle was a social worker in France who shared the same birthday as Lou Gehrig. In fact, Jean was also the exact same height and weight as the Iron Horse. At forty-eight, Jean was stricken with Lou Gehrig's disease and died on the same day the Yankee great did. Of course, the French don't really follow baseball, so everyone just said he died of amyotrophic lateral sclerosis.

Last May 19, Chris Albers went to the Cloverleaf Mall in Medford, Oregon, and parked in space 219. Amazingly, at the very same moment in the Cloverleaf Mall in Duluth, Minnesota, a man also named Chris Albers parked in space 219. The only one aware of this odd coincidence, however, was God.

UNUSED AUDIO COMMENTARY BY HOWARD ZINN AND NOAM CHOMSKY, RECORDED SUMMER 2002, FOR *THE LORD OF THE RINGS: THE FELLOWSHIP OF THE RING* DVD (PLATINUM SERIES EXTENDED EDITION), PART ONE

Jeff Alexander and Tom Bissell

CHOMSKY: The film opens with Galadriel speaking. "The world has changed," she tells us. "I can feel it in the water." She's actually stealing a line from the nonhuman Treebeard. He says this to Merry and Pippin in *The Two Towers,* the novel. Already we can see who is going to be privileged by this narrative and who is not.

ZINN: Of course. "The world has changed." I would argue that the main thing one learns when one watches this film is that the world hasn't changed. Not at all.

CHOMSKY: We should examine carefully what's being established here in the prologue. For one, the point is clearly made that the "master ring," the so-called "one ring to rule them all," is actually a rather elaborate justification for preemptive war on Mordor.

ZINN: I think that's correct. Tolkien makes no attempt to hide the fact that rings are wielded by every other ethnic enclave in Middle Earth. The Dwarves have seven rings, the Elves have three. The race of Man has nine rings, for God's sake. There are at least nineteen rings floating around out there in Middle Earth, and yet Sauron's ring is supposedly so terrible that no one can be allowed to wield it. Why?

CHOMSKY: Notice too that the "war" being waged here is, evidently, in the land of Mordor itself—at the very base of Mount Doom. These terrible armies of Sauron, these dreadful demonized Orcs, have not proved very successful at conquering the neighboring realms—if that is even what Sauron was seeking to do. It seems fairly far-fetched.

ZINN: And observe the map device here—how the map is itself completely Gondor-centric. Rohan and Gondor are treated as though they are the literal center of Middle Earth. Obviously this is because they have men living there. What of places such as Anfalas and Forlindon or Near Harad? One never really hears anything about places like that. And this so-called map casually reveals other places—the Lost Realm, the Northern Waste (lost to whom? wasted how? I ask)—but tells us nothing about them. It is as though the people who live in these places are despicable, and unworthy of mention. Who is producing this tale? What is their agenda? What are their interests and how are those interests being served by this portrayal? Questions we need to ask repeatedly.

CHOMSKY: And here comes Bilbo Baggins. Now, this is, to my mind, where the story begins to reveal its deeper truths. In the books we learn that Saruman was spying on Gandalf for years. And he wondered why Gandalf was traveling so incessantly to the Shire. As Tolkien later establishes, the Shire's surfeit of pipe-weed is one of the major reasons for Gandalf's continued visits.

ZINN: You view the conflict as being primarily about pipe-weed, do you not?

CHOMSKY: Well, what we see here, in Hobbiton, is farmers tilling crops. The thing to remember is that the crop they are tilling is, in fact, pipe-weed, an addictive drug transported and sold throughout Middle Earth for great profit. Without the pipe-weed, Middle Earth would fall apart. Saruman is trying to break up Gandalf's pipe-weed ring. He's trying to divert it.

ZINN: Well, you know, it would be manifestly difficult to believe in magic rings unless everyone was high on pipe-weed. So it is in Gandalf's interest to keep Middle Earth hooked.

CHOMSKY: How do you think these wizards build gigantic towers and mighty fortresses? Where do they get the money? Keep in mind that I do not especially regard anyone, Saruman included, as an agent for progressivism. But obviously the pipe-weed operation that exists is the dominant influence in Middle Earth. It's not some ludicrous magical ring.

ZINN: Gandalf is deeply implicated. That's true. And of course the ring lore begins with him. He's the one who leaks this news of the supposed evil ring.

CHOMSKY: Now here, just before Bilbo's eleventy-first birthday party, we can see some of the symptoms of addiction. We are supposed to attribute Bilbo's tiredness, his sensation of feeling like too little butter spread out on a piece of bread, to this magical ring he supposedly has. It's clear something else may be at work here.... Here we have Pippin and Merry stealing a bunch of fireworks and setting them off. This might be closer to the true heart of the Hobbits.

ZINN: You mean the Hobbits' natural inclination?

CHOMSKY: I think the Hobbits are criminals, essentially.

ZINN: It also seems incredibly irresponsible for Gandalf to have a firework that powerful just sitting in the back of his wagon.

CHOMSKY: Now we come to Bilbo's disappearance. Again, we have to question the validity of the ring and the magic powers attributed to it. Did Bilbo Baggins really disappear at his party, or is this some kind of mass hallucination attributable to a group of intoxicated Hobbits? When forced to consider so-called magic compared to the hallucinatory properties of a known narcotic, Occam's razor would indicate the latter as a far more plausible explanation.

ZINN: And here we receive our first glimpse of the supposedly dreadful Mordor, which actually looks like a fairly functioning place.

CHOMSKY: This type of city is most likely the best the Orcs can do if all they have are cliffs to grow on. It's very impressive, in that sense.

ZINN: Especially considering the economic sanctions no doubt faced by Mordor. They must be dreadful. We see now that the Black Riders have been released, and they're going after Frodo. The Black Riders. Of course they're black. Everything evil is always black. And later Gandalf the Grey becomes Gandalf the White. Have you noticed that?

CHOMSKY: The most simplistic color symbolism.

ZINN: And the writing on the ring, we learn here, is Orcish—the so-called black speech. Orcish is evidently some spoliation of the language spoken in Rohan. This is what Tolkien says.

CHOMSKY: From what I understand, Orcish is a patois that the Orcs developed during their enslavement by Rohan, before they rebelled and left.

ZINN: Well, supposedly the Orcs were first bred by "the dark power of the north in the elder days." Tolkien says that Orc comes from the Mannish word *tark,* which means "man of Gondor."

CHOMSKY: Shameless, really.

ZINN: Gandalf mentions the evil stirring in Mordor. That's all he has to say. "It's evil." He doesn't elaborate on what's going on in Mordor, what the people are going through. They're evil because they're there.

CHOMSKY: I think the fact that we never actually see the enemy is quite damning. Then again, Gandalf is the greatest storyteller of all. He weaves the tales that strand Middle Earth in this state of perpetual conflict.

ZINN: And now Frodo and Sam are joined by Merry and Pippin, as they finally escape the Shire. They're being chased by the Black Riders. Again, if these Black Riders are so fearsome, and they can smell the ring so vividly, why don't they ever seem able to find the Hobbits when they're standing right next to them?

CHOMSKY: This episode in Bree should cause us to ask, too, how much Frodo knows about the conspiracy. He seems to be piecing it together a little bit. I think at first he's an unwitting participant, fooled by Gandalf's propaganda.

ZINN: I'm much more suspicious of Frodo than you are. I've always viewed him as one of the most malevolent actors in this drama, precisely because of how he abets people like Gandalf. He uses a fake name, Mr. Underhill, just as Gandalf goes by several names: Mithrandir, the Grey Pilgrim, the White Rider. Strider is also Aragorn, is also Estel, is also Elessar, is also Dunadan. He has all these identities.

CHOMSKY: We call those aliases today.

ZINN: But is Sauron ever anything but Sauron? Is Saruman ever anything but Saruman?

CHOMSKY: And now, with Frodo in the midst of a hallucinogenic, paranoid state, we meet Strider.

ZINN: A ranger. I believe today we call them serial killers.

CHOMSKY: Or drug smugglers.

ZINN: And notice how Strider characterizes the Black Riders. "Neither living nor dead." Why, that's a really useful enemy to have.

CHOMSKY: Yes. In this way you can never verify their existence, and yet they're horribly terrifying. We should not overlook the fact that Middle Earth is in a cold war at this moment, locked in perpetual conflict. Strider's rhetoric serves to keep fear alive.

ZINN: You've spoken to me before about Mordor's lack of access to the mineral wealth that the Dwarves control.

CHOMSKY: If we're going to get into the socioeconomic reasons why certain structures develop in certain cultures … it's mainly geographical. We have Orcs in Mordor—trapped, with no mineral resources—hemmed in by the Ash Mountains, where the "free peoples" of Middle Earth can put a city, like Osgiliath, and effectively keep the border closed.

ZINN: Don't forget the Black Gate. The Black Gate, which, as Tolkien points out, was built by Gondor. And now we jump to the Orcs chopping down the trees in Isengard.

CHOMSKY: A terrible thing the Orcs do here, isn't it? They destroy nature. But again, what have we seen, time and time again?

ZINN: The Orcs have no resources. They're desperate.

CHOMSKY: Desperate people driven to do desperate things.

ZINN: Desperate to compete with the economic powerhouses of Rohan and Gondor.

CHOMSKY: Who really knows their motive? Maybe this is a means to an end. And while that might not be the best philosophy in the world, it makes the race of Man in no way superior. They're going to great lengths to hold on to their power. Two cultures locked in conflict over power, with one culture clearly suffering a great deal. I think sharing power and resources would have been the wisest approach, but Rohan and Gondor have shown no interest in doing so. Sometimes, revolution must be—

ZINN: Mistakes are often—

CHOMSKY: Blood must be shed. I forget what Thomas Jefferson—

ZINN: He said that blood was the—

CHOMSKY: The blood of tyrants—

ZINN: The blood of tyrants—

CHOMSKY: —waters the tree of—

ZINN: —revolution.

CHOMSKY: —freedom. Or revolution. Something like that.

ZINN: I think that's actually very, very close.

CHOMSKY: I think this is a tragedy, this story. Because it's about two cultures. And poor leadership. It's a human tragedy, and an Orcish tragedy.

ZINN: A perfect example of what you're talking about is right here, when Strider attacks the Black Riders, "saving" Frodo from them.

CHOMSKY: Think of it from the Black Riders' perspective. No doubt they arrived at Weathertop thinking, "Can we ask a few questions? We'd like to talk to you."

ZINN: Now from here we jump to Isengard, post–ecological atrocities. What I personally see here is … well, I see industrialization, I see a very cooperative workforce, I see a people who aren't terrorized, a people attempting to make do with what they have.

CHOMSKY: Well, they're making weapons, which is sad. I mean, it would be nice if they could make plowshares, but unfortunately this isn't the time for plowshares in their culture. But they're showing great ingenuity, and they're showing cooperation, you're right about that.

ZINN: Actually it shows the Orcs smithing a lot of pieces of metal. I don't think it's necessarily established that what they're making is swords, is it? They could be farming implements of some sort. They're definitely unusual-looking. But I have to ask you, what about the genetic engineering that goes on with the Uruk-hai?

CHOMSKY: It's certainly a strange aspect of their culture, but why should we be so condemning? I mean, this is the way they reproduce. If it looks disgusting to us, well maybe we should readjust what we regard as disgusting. I mean, is that any more vile than pulling a baby out of a gaping, bloody hole?

ZINN: Now we witness the Black Riders finally together—all nine Riders—giving chase to Arwen and Frodo. When we see the Orcs destroy their environment, it is this big scandal. But Arwen is able to send a whole herd of watery horses down a river, no doubt a very delicate ecosystem, and probably completely demolish it, and no one says anything about that.

CHOMSKY: The Elves, of course, always say that they are the best custodians of nature. And there's a curious type of nature-worship in their culture that allows them to claim, by every implication, "Trees are more important than people." They don't regard the Orcs as people. However, Orcs are thinking, sentient, conscious beings with a culture and a language. They feel pain. They express emotion. They are constantly evolving, trying to better themselves.

ZINN: But here the Elvish culture is revealed to be very elaborate, because, of course, they have better architecture. But I vastly prefer the real grittiness one finds in Mordor. Think of the suspiciously clean city of Rivendell. You don't see any life going on there. No people at all. There's hardly anyone in the streets. It should be said, though, that, on occasion, the Orcs have been known to eat one another.

CHOMSKY: That's cannibalism, sure, but maybe it's part of a sacred ritual with them. Maybe it's an ancient part of their culture. Who are we to judge? Still, I have problems with it, I agree.

ZINN: So here we have another shot of Rivendell being beautiful because it happens to be located in the mountains, where the lighter people live.

CHOMSKY: The humans are all so entranced by the Elves' completely mythological power. It's a spell that has been cast upon them.

ZINN: I see the humans, embodied by Aragorn, as being indicative of a sort of middle-class longing.

CHOMSKY: It keeps them striving. If you're a good enough man, you can be an Elf.

ZINN: An Elf. As if that's the best thing to be.

CHOMSKY: Now, at the Council of Elrond, we have the Middle Earth equivalent of a television broadcast. It's one guy sitting in a tall chair and talking at twenty other people. This is how information is spread in this culture. But, you know, it doesn't have to be this way. Imagine that, right now, you have the people in Gondor with a palantir, the people in Rohan with a palantir, the people in the Woodland Realm with a palantir. And everyone could be standing around it, talking to one another, sharing a conference in which the people have an equal interest and stake in what decisions are made.

ZINN: Technology that Gandalf already knows is available. But do we see a single Orc?

CHOMSKY: Oh, of course not. Of course not. Because everyone here has a vested interest in keeping the Orcs down.

ZINN: Boromir is the only one honest enough to talk about what the real story is here.

CHOMSKY: Boromir's an interesting case. His culture is threatened by the Orcs in a very real way. But he's also seen that this occupation of Orc land is engendered by his people's own aggressive policies. So he's like an enlightened Israeli who looks at the situation and says, "If I were in their situation, I would be just like them."

ZINN: Now Frodo, son of Drogo, agrees to take the ring to Mount Doom. Something tells me that no one in Mordor calls it Mount Doom.

CHOMSKY: And everyone baits Frodo into this. "You are our agent, going on a suicide mission. You have to do it for the Motherland."

ZINN: So is Frodo the Mohammed Atta figure in this story?

CHOMSKY: He's a fanatical true believer. And crazy. Obviously, totally insane.

ZINN: And listen to what Aragorn tells Frodo: "You have my sword."

CHOMSKY: So militaristic.

ZINN: I think the only real diplomat of Middle Earth is Gollum. He's the only one who makes any meaningful, cross-cultural exchange with any of these people: being a torture victim at the hand of the Orcs, and his attempted strangulation of the Hobbits.

CHOMSKY: I think of Gollum as more of a deluded madman, one more sinned against than sinning.

ZINN: There's room for argument. And, yet again, here we see Bilbo ravaged from the effects of pipe-weed. It's been flushed from his system in his idyll-cum-rehab in Rivendell. And what does he give Frodo? He gives him his sword, of course. Sting.

CHOMSKY: As if to say, "You know, when you've stabbed enough people in the back like I have, you'll need this shirt of mithril." Hobbits are bandits. They have this little veneer of nobility around them, but they are nothing more than demented little thieves.

ZINN: On the way to Moria, here, we should point out the fear that men and Elves have of the Dwarves' culture. They refuse to enter the mines of Moria.

CHOMSKY: There is something very funny lingering around the edges of the whole Moria episode. Could it be that the Dwarves living there were starting to get different ideas about the Orcs? Were starting to talk to the Orcs, and establish some means of cross-cultural communication? Perhaps Gandalf and some of his Rohan friends went there only to find a bunch of Dwarves and Orcs talking, maybe forming an alliance or pact. And then Gandalf massacred all of them, and pretended as though there was some huge battle. This would explain why Gandalf can't lead them back there. Genocide's been committed. He hasn't yet weaved a good enough story to explain away the evidence. He has to pretend that Moria is this scary place.

ZINN: Now, we see in Moria that the Dwarves had a fairly sophisticated mithril mine here. Wouldn't you say the Dwarves are the Jew-like figures of Middle Earth?

CHOMSKY: They are former slaves. The comparison is apt.

ZINN: They're good at doing things with their hands. This is something Tolkien is very adamant about. They're useful, but they're not very educated. Ah, and this is also where we first see Gollum. I stick to my view of Gollum as a rebel who transgresses boundaries. In many ways he is the heroic, empathetic conscience of this story. He's the only one who cares about bridging the gaps between these many cultures.

CHOMSKY: You could be right. I think there's possibly something very wise about Gollum. Obviously he's well-traveled; he's a hermit.

ZINN: I think his sexuality is questionable, and that's why he's viewed as this hateful, awful thing. Everyone always talks about killing him.

CHOMSKY: Gandalf of course likes to have as many ghosts around him as possible. He slyly encourages Frodo in this belief that Gollum is some kind of horrible, corrupt thing. He neglects to say, "You know, I tortured him just a couple of weeks ago."

ZINN: Exactly.

CHOMSKY: Notice that Gandalf doesn't give anybody else the supposed Dwarf book to read. Gandalf could be passing it off as Balin's last words. We don't know what is actually recorded in it, though. Very cunning. It could be an agreement drawn up between the Orcs and the Dwarves. It could quite easily be that.

ZINN: It would explain why he kept it out of Gimli's hands.

CHOMSKY: Sure. "No, don't worry. I'll read it. Let me read this to you guys."

ZINN: This is much more of a Gandalfian, flowery language. It's hard to imagine the Dwarves writing that way.

CHOMSKY: And now the terrible Orcs invade Balin's tomb. Let's be clear about a few things here. The Orcs are fighting a war of self-defense against the invading Fellowship. They basically busted in on the Orcs' place here. It's fairly clear that the Orcs are hiding there because if they go outside they have every reason to believe that they will be massacred by Gandalf.

ZINN: The Orcs certainly don't seem to be very good fighters, do they? If they're such a terrible, evil, warlike culture—

CHOMSKY: They can't kill even one of these little Hobbits who just received their swords only a few days ago. One would think that if the Orcs were as bad as the corrupt Man-Elf coalition says, they would be a lot better at fighting. It lends credence to the farming hypothesis—that they were trying to scrabble out a meager existence in the land in Mordor.

ZINN: Here, very significantly, we have the Bridge of Khazad-Dûm. You will notice that what is destroyed is a bridge—another potential connector.

CHOMSKY: On a symbolic level, that is a very good point.

ZINN: All the borders in this film are constantly being destroyed, or overrun, or eliminated, or sealed. It's all about fear—fearing the other. Notice, too, that the Elf Legolas jumps across the ruined bridge first.

CHOMSKY: They'll cross this bridge and the bridge will collapse, and they'll never be able to communicate with the Balrog again, or with the Orcs inside. In fact, they're sealing off the Orcs from ever escaping. They're leaving the Orcs in the cave with this big Balrog. Now, again, surely, among these Moria Orcs were some Orc radicals—aggressive, angry, militant radicals. We shouldn't understate that.

ZINN: Well, look how the Orcs grow up. What do you expect?

CHOMSKY: I mean, what other options have they?

ZINN: I dare say that, were I an Orc, I might possibly be one of those terrorist Orcs, shooting arrows at the Fellowship myself.

CHOMSKY: Here comes the Balrog. Notice Gandalf's unilateral action. "Quick, get away, I have to fight this thing alone!"

ZINN: Once again you see a creature that's on fire being demonized in this movie: the flaming eye, the flaming Balrog. As though being on fire is this terrible affliction to have.

CHOMSKY: As though they can help it if they're on fire.

ZINN: After Gandalf falls, you get another view of the so-called terrorist Orcs. You know, the regrettable side of the Orcs does occasionally come out. The violence. It doesn't help their cause when these distinct, individual Orcs take it upon themselves to lash out at the inequality of the system. But notice that even these violent Orcs don't seem happy. They're not pleased with themselves. It's a violence born of necessity.

CHOMSKY: Sure. They're trapped in a cycle of violence.

ZINN: And now we come to Galadriel's wood, Lothlorien. Look at how the Elves greet people—with arrows. Is that so different from the Orcs?

CHOMSKY: Right. And they're supposed to be nature-worshipers. It's sort of sickening and very bourgeois. Have you taken proper note of Galadriel's farewell gesture, when the Fellowship sets its boats down the Silverlode? It is some sort of "sieg heil" gesture.

ZINN: It is vaguely reminiscent of the biomechanics of National Socialism. You'll notice, too, how clearly the Man-Elf coalition controls all the modes of transportation in Middle Earth. We always see the Orcs running. But Legolas, Gimli, and Aragorn—I mean, sometimes they are riding horses. The Orcs have nothing like any of this. The Orcs certainly don't canoe.

CHOMSKY: Well, they don't have these wide, beautiful rivers to canoe on. That's part of the deprivation of their natural resources. And just as you say, here the Orcs are, running. A bunch of farmers, holding their clumsy weapons.

ZINN: Good lord, these giant statues on the Anduin River. The Sentinels of Númenor. These huge, monolithic statues that have their hands thrust forever up. I think I can intuit what these sentinels are saying: "Stay away, Orcs."

CHOMSKY: "Keep out of our land."

ZINN: I have to ask, what does this story do for the powerful? For one, it makes them feel very good about the kind of things they've done to less powerful societies. The way they exploit them and the way they invent these phony pretexts to wage wars of aggression against less powerful people. The powerful need to tell themselves these stories.

CHOMSKY: And yet, as in all stories of this type, hidden within the story are the keys to unlocking the hidden modes of power.

ZINN: The thing is, though, that even when the dominant culture tells itself the story, the story cannot help but include those telltale signifiers of power that surrender the true nature of the story.

CHOMSKY: It is embedded, I would say, in the language of the story itself. No matter how often the storytellers try to obscure the truth, the truth will out. The truth will be betrayed through the way the story gets told.

ZINN: Thankfully, the literature of oppression can never last because the oppression is always so obvious. It's always about the people who are suppressed, who keep getting more and more aware of how they're suppressed. And once they're aware of how suppressed they are, they can—

CHOMSKY: Right, they're able to—

ZINN: We've got to get our conspiracy straight.

CHOMSKY: Not necessarily. Think of Lee Harvey Oswald.

ZINN: A patsy. A CIA agent.

CHOMSKY: A cold-blooded, ruthless killer.

ZINN: Right.

CHOMSKY: He was a good shot. He was a bad shot.

ZINN: Right. Exactly.

CHOMSKY: But then, I don't really believe in conspiracy theories about JFK.

ZINN: Neither do I.

CHOMSKY: So.

ZINN: Isn't that funny?

CANCELED REGIONAL MORNING TV SHOWS

John Moe

Hot Coffee Thrown in Houston's Face
The Fort Wayne Morning Shed
Shame on You, Denver!
Tulsa Kills Itself
Why Won't You Love Me, Cincinnati?
A.M. Terrified Grin Detroit
The Ghost of Anwar Sadat Inexplicably Haunts Tacoma
Wake the Hell Up, Knoxville
Please, Phoenix, Let's Never Speak of This Again
Uncomfortable Portland Morning with the Sweaty Guy
I'm Sick of You, Wichita. I'm Sick of You and I'm Sick of Your Shit.
Billings Might As Well Be Dead
Boston Morning with Stabby and Shouty
Orlando Angst
I Said Wake the Hell Up, Knoxville! Jesus!
Percodan-Free Pittsburgh
Get Off Me, Atlanta!
Crispin Glover's Biloxi Morning Zoo
Wake Up, Mommy! Mommy? Baltimore
Johnny Cocktail's Salt Lake City Morning Lounge
What's the Point, Duluth?
God Hates Anchorage. He Told Me.
Bryant Gumbel Is Pissed Off Again, New York
Knoxville, I'm Gonna Whup Your Ass If You Don't Wake Up!
Good Morning, Indiancrapolis

A LETTER FROM EZRA POUND
TO BILLY WILDER, 1963
Greg Purcell

Dear Animal,

Your sect'y makes some faint excuse for your continued incivility and your putrid meanness in not returning my original mss.; i.e., of the screen adaptation I have made of *The Aeneid,* to be played, as per my suggestion, by Charlton Heston. As everything concerning this project has, in my mind, completely fallen apart, I can ask for nothing but that the screenplay be returned to me post haste, and in its original form.

I suppose it is possible that, in the depth of your alcoholic stupidity, you may have glossed over or, worse, forgotten the reservations I am having about this project. I elaborate them here again, as I am always doing for the benefit of children such as yourself. They are as follows:

To begin with, your hold on Latin is deplorable. I suppose you've found it necessary to peddle this film to an American audience, and to therefore impurify it by rendering it into English. But to have translated it yourself! Wilder, the refrain goes "mirabile dictu!," not "miserabile dictu!"

Though, in your hands, I'm beginning to suspect that Virgil's tale will indeed be more wretched than wonderful to tell. You have also mangled the first line, obviously confusing *virumque* with *virorum*. The poet is clearly not singing "about the men's arms." You are an idiot.

Secondly, I have suggested CHARLTON HESTON for this role, not Jack Lemmon, as you have suggested. To cast Jack Lemmon in the role is patently absurd. Perhaps he may find a place in the screen adaptation of Juvenal's Satires I am currently rendering for John Ford (who, I might add, is a superior director to you). Now, you see, the Satires—that's comedy. There is a bit of broad slapstick in the work, at the like of which this Lemmon character seems reductively adept, as when Juvenal is walking down the paved streets of Nero's Rome and finds nothing there but litter and human excrement piled up in the alleyways. That, as you might say, is "blue-chip stuff," or whatever it is that you people call it when you're jabbering away about nothing at all. Really, you are like a monkey or an ape to me. Monkeys and apes should not be allowed access to works as great as *The Aeneid*.

Thirdly, I will not, I repeat, WILL NOT introduce the movie dressed in a tweed suit coat, sitting in an oak-lined drawing room, with an impossibly large book in my lap. I also dislike the introduction of the "helmeted skeleton army" on page 53.

Elia Kazan says you are supposed to be ill. I hope you are. And what is more I hope you die of it. In the meantime return my mss., crawl out of the thief category, and make peace with whatever diseased deity is provided for such bacilli as yourself.

Damn you again, and may three new lice hatch eggs on your already infected scalp. May you also vomit on cave-treacle.

Yrs candidly,
EZRA

JOURNAL OF A NEW COBRA RECRUIT

Keith Pille

May 1, 1986
Man. I'm so excited to graduate this month. It's been a fun few weeks, signing yearbooks and going to beer parties and such, but at the same time I keep feeling worried about what I'm going to do afterwards. I don't have the grades for college. Heck, when I talked to the Army recruiter about becoming a G.I., he said I don't even have the grades to serve my country. I sure don't want to work at the gas station like my brother.

May 2, 1986
Today this guy in a blue uniform came up and gave me a pamphlet. Said he was a recruiter for COBRA, an outfit a lot like the Army but without all those government regulations to slow down the fun. We talked a little and he said he liked the cut of my jib, thought I'd be great COBRA material.

May 15, 1986

Signed up with COBRA today. I got real excited when they said I earned a signing bonus ... figured it would be a couple hundred bucks that I could put toward a new bumper for my truck. Nope. Just a T-shirt with a funny-looking snake on the front. And I'm not supposed to wear it in public. Pretty weird stuff, but they seem like nice guys. I report to COBRA boot camp out in Utah in the middle of June. The recruiter guy said that everyone around there thinks it's where some crazy old Mormon lives with all his wives. I'm not supposed to say anything about it to anyone. I'm supposed to tell Mom and Dad that I'm going off to work for the phone company.

June 16, 1986

First day of boot camp was a bear. All of the other boots seem like nice guys. Don't know what any of them look like because the first thing they did when we got here was give us blue helmets with black hankies to cover up our faces. I'm getting pretty good at recognizing people's eyebrows though.

Figured we'd do a lot of exercise today, but we didn't do as much as I thought. Mostly just running out of a door and yelling "COBRA!" at the top of our lungs. I got pretty good at it. Now I can sound awful scary when I yell "COBRA!" You wouldn't think it would wear you down, but boy, am I pooped.

June 18, 1986

Boot camp's still a lot of fun. And I'm learning a lot. Today we did more mental learning stuff than exercise. We received a lecture about our main enemy, the G.I. Joe team. Seems that Uncle Sam is so nervous about COBRA that he set up an elite team of soldiers just to try to fight us. I couldn't be more proud. I had no idea I was signing on with a bunch that was this important. I guess the Joes have stopped us at pretty much everything we've ever tried to do. But believe me, is that going to change now that Steve Loring is a member of COBRA!

Sarge said all kinds of funny things about how dumb the G.I. Joe team is. Like, they just have one person who's good at each thing they do. So they just have one guy who can fly a plane, and one guy who knows how to drive a tank, one guy who can fly a helicopter, one guy who can fight in the desert, and so on. They even have a whole aircraft carrier (for their one plane and one helicopter) with just a captain and one sailor to run it! Sarge was like, "What the heck kind of outfit is that?" and we were all just in stitches. Then this one recruit (I think it was Renfro, but I didn't get a good look at his eyebrows) says, "But if they're so dumb, how come they always beat us?"

Sarge made Renfro go out and run around the track and yell "COBRA!" for an hour.

June 20, 1986

Real boring day. I was all ready for some more physical training, but instead Sarge led us into a room full of phones and made us cold-call people and ask them if they wanted to switch their long distance to COBRA. During the break, Renfro asked Sarge when we became a long-distance provider. Sarge explained that we had to do something to make money if we were going to afford a private army with hundreds of tanks and planes and a Terrordome, not to mention all the expenses from the Serpentor genetic engineering project. Working the phones was demoralizing, and people were usually pretty mad when we called them, but it felt good to be doing my duty for COBRA. In between calls, I amused myself by thinking of cool one-liners I could say if I ever got the drop on one of those G.I. Joe bums.

June 21, 1986

Awful exciting day today. First we got to do our airborne training. They loaded us up into a plane, and we flew up and then jumped out. Our chutes had the big, scary COBRA symbol on them. It was awesome. But it was hard, because we were supposed to keep yelling "COBRA!" all the way down. It was tough to get enough breath to yell right at first. Sarge says it just takes practice.

After that we finally got to do weapons training. About time! They gave me a rifle and pointed at the target. I held the rifle up to my cheek and sighted down the barrel, just like I did when I went deer hunting with Grampa. Boy, did Sarge go apeshit over that! Got in my face and started yelling at me, asking how I expected to scare someone if I just stood there all quiet-like and shot so carefully.

Sarge is a great teacher because he doesn't just criticize. He showed the right way to shoot. What you do is you start shooting your gun wildly and run toward the target as fast as you can and, in your scariest voice, you yell "COBRA!" We worked on that all afternoon, and just before we broke for dinner, I actually hit the target! Sarge and everyone else were so happy for me that they were about to cry. Told me I'd just set the record for marksmanship in COBRA boot camp. I wanted to call Mom and tell her the good news, but she thinks I work for the phone company.

June 22, 1986

First payday. No check, just a couple more of those T-shirts. Doughty and me planned to drive into town and sell the shirts for spending money, but Sarge caught wind of our plan, reminding us that we weren't supposed to let anyone see the T-shirts because then they'd know we were in COBRA.

June 25, 1986

Tank training today! Wow, it was great! They didn't let us drive the HISS tanks ourselves, but we got to practice riding in the back turret and working the guns. By now we all knew what we were supposed to do without being told, and Sarge said he was so proud at the way we all just yelled "COBRA!" and shot wildly before he even showed us how.

Renfro tried to ruin the day with a whole bunch of his questions. First he asked Sarge why our combat fatigues were sky blue, saying we're visible from a mile away at least. Then, when we were practicing with the HISS tanks, Renfro started in on why the HISS driver wasn't protected by anything more than a piece of glass. And for that matter, he continued, why do we run the guns from an open turret with no protection at all? Sarge just about blew up. I think Renfro's going to be running around the track and yelling "COBRA!" for a long, long time tonight.

A LOGIC PUZZLE
AND HANGOVER CURE

John Hodgman

1.

There is a room with seven chairs in it.

Eight people are standing in the room.

Some of them are Vampires.

Some of them are Normals.

Vampires always lie.

Normals always tell the truth.

The room has three enormous windows in it, all facing west.

It is six o'clock on an October evening.

Sunset may be seen through the westward windows. It is
     magnificent.

(By the way, the Vampires have been awake all day. The sun
     does not kill them. They're not that kind of Vampires.)

The Vampires are very handsome and very beautiful at the
     same time.

They only tell handsome and beautiful lies.

The Normals are wandering around the room, spreading vicious truths wherever they go.

There are two large bottles of inexpensive wine on the table, one of which is poisoned, one of which is not.

Also, you are ruinously drunk.

Either a Vampire or a Normal touches your shoulder and suggests something that surprises you.

It begins as a statement and ends as a question.

Without feeling for fangs, and lying or telling the truth as you see fit, what three questions and two statements do you pose in order to determine whether you are standing or sitting down?

Hint: The wine is rosé.

2.

Combine the yolk of one egg with four ounces of flat club soda.

Add milk and vodka (warm) to taste.

Rent *The Seven Samurai* and begin watching it.

Drink the yolk/soda/milk/vodka combination while watching Tape One of *The Seven Samurai,* rubbing bare feet on the carpet.

Upon conclusion of Tape One, decide to take a shower, then change your mind.

Prepare a box of instant mashed potatoes as directed. Add one whole bottle of Tabasco and the juice of one lemon.

While mixing, remember high school until it becomes too painful to continue.

While sucking on one ice cube, watch Tape Two of *The Seven Samurai* until conclusion.

Reaffirm your faith that any effort to save a village of peasants from marauding bandits will always end in tragedy.

Sleep for ten hours.

Awaken at sunset and suddenly realize: Everyone is standing, including yourself.
Attempt to explain this to your wife.

If you do not have carpeting, substitute a bath mat or an old coat.

SOME PEOPLE DON'T
LIKE CELEBRITIES

Michael Ian Black

SOME PEOPLE JUST don't like me. I know this is hard to believe, especially when you consider the following:

1. I am a celebrity (very famous).
2. I give sixty percent of my income to "Jerry's Kids."
3. I hardly ever kick my dog.

Two of these things are true, and shouldn't that be enough to ensure me a large measure of goodwill from my fellow man? After all, I harbor no ill will toward anybody (except for that motherfucker Paul Newman—he knows why).

This is why it was so surprising for me to learn that there are people out there, people I have never even met, who do not like me.

I first became aware of this after appearing on the VH1 television program *I Love the 70s*. You may have seen this show. According to the VH1 press release, it's a "fun-filled ride through the music, movies, TV shows, products, fashions, fads, trends, and major events that defined pop culture each year of the decade." Whatever. They paid me two grand.

For people who feel the need to share their thoughts about television shows with complete strangers, VH1 maintains an Internet message board. It was while perusing these boards that I first encountered several dispiriting posts under topics like "Michael Ian Black sucks," "Michael Ian Black—DIE!," and perhaps most painful of all, "Michael Ian Black is not that cute."

Needless to say, I was blown away. I mean, look at me. I'm really cute.

My initial shock soon turned to numbness, followed by denial, anger, depression, a brief moment of total euphoria, and then back to depression.

I have decided to share some of those messages here, in an effort to confront the final stage in my grieving process: acceptance. Not to sound egotistical, but it is my hope that by accepting and honoring the writers' feelings, I will not only heal myself, but will also literally heal the world.

*   *   *

From keithpartridge:

"[Michael Ian Black is] the most arrogant, self-absorbed, uninteresting, pretentious, cynical human being with no talent that VH1 ever hired to talk about something they have no knowledge about whatsoever ..."

(The grammar might be a touch clunky, Keith, but your message rings loud and clear. I honor your feelings. Well said.)

*   *   *

From Maddmaxx14:

"What does this snotnosed little **** think he knows about the 70s"

(The asterisks are Maddmaxx14's, not mine. I don't know what they stood for, but I think it was probably "faggot." Thanks for having the class not to say it, Madd.)

*   *   *

From Hollandscomet:

"how long after his lobotomy did they tape his segments, anyway?!? This guy has all the personality of a doorstop!"

(Not to quibble, but there are some really whimsical doorstops on the market. Check out avalongarden.com for the "green rabbit" and "butch" doorstops; they've got personality in spades. Your point, however, is taken.)

*   *   *

From Born2Soon:

"MIB was crass enough to say that Arnold from *Diff'rent Strokes* should have been on *Roots*. Why? He didn't say why."

(The reason I thought Arnold should play Kunta Kinte is so he could say, "Whatchu talkin' 'bout, Master?" which I thought would be cute. Sorry about the confusion. I should have made this clearer.)

*   *   *

Another from Born2Soon:

"MIB looks like he's had botox on his forehead. His forehead never moves, even when he moves his eyebrows or smiles, which is rarely.... He most likely had it done due to VANITY. That's the usual reason."

(It's true. I have had some work done, specifically in the forehead region. Vanity, however, wasn't the reason. It was because I was horribly burned in a fire.)

From Penlane 40:

"I was fast-forwarding through his comments after he said Benji and his girlfriend didn't do it doggy style ... what an idiot!"

(I did indeed feel like an idiot after speaking to a number of veterinarians and learning that the only way Benji and his girlfriend could possibly have "done it" was doggy style. Mea culpa.)

*   *   *

There are, of course, more. Hundreds more. To those people, and to the thousands more who did not have the courage to write, I want to say this: I am really, really, really, really, really sorry. There aren't enough "really"'s to convey how sorry I am. Further, know this: I have learned from this experience, and I have changed.

I only hope these same people will accept and support me on my next television project, *Albert Schweitzer Can Suck Me,* in which I use my winning sense of humor to rip the famed humanitarian a new asshole.

TIPS FROM *JOKES AND HOW TO TELL THEM,* PUBLISHED IN 1963

R. J. White

In this story, it's the chimpanzee who has dignity.

You may not like the name "Jonquil," but I do; that's just a personal choice.

The waiter should sound just a shade British.

Moses and God are very matter-of-fact in their dialogue, a wee bit Bronxy.

The bird, a tough guy, has learned his English watching TV serials.

There is nothing to be done about joyboy.

If you're telling this story out of the United States, better use Eisenhower.

To my knowledge, this story presents the only fallible ghost I've ever heard of.

Try to imagine the late Charles Laughton telling that one.

The policeman, of course, pantomimes his golf instructions at the end.

When the brother teaches the man to say "chicken sandwich," he should articulate it very slowly.

The zebra wouldn't be in pajamas, nor would the stallion think she was in them, it being broad daylight.

As in any story dealing with a mental aberration, the patient is very serious and you, the storyteller, do not make fun of them.

Also, it should be quite clear in your opening description that the Rabbi knows he's doing wrong but can't resist the urge.

The man in the gallery should cup his hands to his mouth and bellow the punch line.

The horse is just astonished as he blurts out his final line.

HOW IMPORTANT MOMENTS IN MY LIFE WOULD HAVE BEEN DIFFERENT IF I WAS SHOT TWICE IN THE STOMACH

Jake Swearingen

BIRTH
The doctor tells my mother to push while she also tells the nurse to get my father. My mother has been in labor for nearly forty hours. My father rushes into the room, his face a mix of pure terror and pure joy. I come out, nearly dead from blood loss. I appear on both *Oprah* and *Donahue,* being the only person ever shot twice in the stomach while still in the womb.

WALKING FOR THE FIRST TIME
I stand up on shaky, little-boy legs, and then promptly fall over, a pool of my own blood spreading out from underneath me.

FIRST DAY OF SCHOOL
I walk in, nervous and scared and wishing I could go back home, and then stumble backward, clutching my stomach. "Aw, Christ! Aw, shit!" I say as I knock over a chair, looking

down as dark blood seeps from between my fingers. I make three new friends that day.

FIRST KISS
She is the girl in my Business Tech class from school, and we have met in the recreation room of my church. She is wearing some sort of fruity perfume, and her hair is tied back. I lean forward, and my breath is coming in shaky little gasps. Our lips touch, and then I cough twice, blood slowly leaking out of my mouth. I ask her to call an ambulance, goddamnit, I've been fucking shot. I sob quietly that I don't want to die here.

GRADUATION
I walk across the stage and shake the principal's hand while he hands me my diploma. I collapse a few steps after, and the entire auditorium where graduation is being held goes deadly quiet. All you can hear is my girlish whimpering in pain and begging for someone to just put me out of my misery, for the love of Christ.

FIRST DAY OF COLLEGE
I step into my dorm and greet my new roommate. We talk for a while, learning about each other. I then lurch backward against the wall, a look of shock and pain on my face. My legs buckle beneath me and I slump to the ground, my eyes staring off into nothing, but suddenly I don't look to be in pain. I look peaceful and almost happy, and I whisper, right before I go, "It's not the end, is it?"

GETTING SHOT IN THE STOMACH AT CLOSE RANGE
This is actually pretty much the same.

NO JUSTICE, NO FOUL
Jim Stallard

WHENEVER I HEAR some historian on PBS prattling about the Supreme Court, I have to step outside for air. I know it's a matter of seconds before the stock phrases—judicial review, legal precedent, activist court—will start rolling out, and I'll feel my blood coming to a boil as I hear the scamming of yet another generation.

Are you sitting down? Everything you were taught about the Supreme Court and its decisions is bunk. For most of the nineteenth century and all of the twentieth, our biggest, most far-reaching legal decisions have been decided not by careful examination of facts and reference to precedent but by contests of game and sport between the justices. The games varied through the years—cribbage, chess, horseshoes, darts—even a brief, disastrous flirtation with polo. (Now do you understand *Plessy v. Ferguson?*) But ever since 1923, basketball has been the only game, and as the years rolled by and the decisions came down, the whole thing has settled nicely into place. Basketball has shaped the way our society is today, every contour, every legality, every way that one person relates to another in an official, sanctioned sense.

I know, I know—you're thinking I got this stuff from radio signals in my head. Actually, the reason I'm privy to this info is really quite mundane. My father was a Supreme Court maintenance worker from 1925 until he retired forty years later. He started sneaking me in to see games when I was eight. I saw my share (though none of the landmarks) and heard from many sources about countless others.

Oliver Wendell Holmes hit on the basketball idea after attending a collegiate game in New York during the Court's Christmas recess in 1922. He thought he had finally identified the type of contest that could involve all the justices, could be played indoors when the Court was in "session," and, most important of all, did not involve horses.

Holmes brought the idea back to Washington and pitched it to Chief Justice Taft. The corpulent chief had been lobbying for Greco-Roman wrestling, but he was starting to realize none of his colleagues would go for a sport in which they might be killed. (The Fatty Arbuckle incident was fresh on everyone's minds.) Taft finally agreed that basketball offered a superior form of jurisprudence.

After a little tinkering, the procedure came down to this: whenever the justices were evenly split over a judgment (four to four with one judge abstaining) and the deadlock persisted for more than a week, the issue would move to the hardwood. In general, the "teams" could be described as liberal vs. conservative, although as court watchers know, legal philosophies cannot be reduced to such simplistic terms. The justice voted most valuable player in the game was allowed the choice of writing the opinion or—in the case of a political hot potato—making someone else do it.

For the first twelve years, the justices scrapped in a dreary gymnasium tucked in the basement of the Capitol building. The floor was cement and the baskets were mounted flush on the walls so that every fast break or layup carried the threat of a concussion. (Owen Roberts became notorious for his short-term memory and was constantly being carried off the floor.)

When the new Court building went up across the street in 1935, the justices insisted that the fourth floor remain mostly vacant to house the real highest court in the land. Because of a mix-up in the architectural plans, the room had a ceiling that was far too low—a fact that made Chief Justice Charles Evans Hughes livid and which has left its imprint on American history: many landmark decisions might have gone differently if the room could have accommodated justices with a high arc on their shot—Stanley Reed, Robert Jackson, and, most tragically, Abe Fortas.

Mind you, everything leading up to the actual decision was, and is, legitimate. The Court still accepted petitions on merit, they still read the briefs, listened (or dozed) during oral argument and then went into conference prepared to vote one way or another. When the deadlock came, however, the bifocals came off and the hightops went on.

Let's look at some of the landmark games, with impressions gleaned from those lucky few who witnessed them:

Near v. Minnesota (1931)

A First Amendment ruling that came down in favor of a sleazy Minnesota newspaper being sued for libel after using ethnic slurs. Charles Evans Hughes (twenty-eight points, thirteen rebounds, seven steals) thought some of the newspaper's comments were pretty funny, so he set out to win the MVP and the opinion that followed. "He was good, and he loved to talk out there," said one observer. "I'm no choirboy, but some of the things he was saying had my face turning red. The ref finally gave him a technical to quiet him down." Hughes's mouth finally got him in trouble in the waning moments. After hitting nothing but net, he pointed at Justice Pierce Butler—a bookish sort who had been the subject of persistent rumors—waited a few beats ... and then yelled "Swish!" The observer recalled, "It was the only time I've ever seen a referee give two technicals at once to the same guy: One, two, gone."

Hirabayashi v. United States (1943) {see fig.1}

The case involved the rights of a Japanese-American citizen as the wartime government was herding his kind around California, but it turned out to be about so much more. Harlan Stone lured Robert Jackson into committing three charging fouls and turned the game around with a steal, a blocked shot, and a wicked bounce pass to Felix Frankfurter that left Owen Roberts and Stanley Reed glued to the floor, their mouths agape. Stone is credited by more than one as the person who remade the legal landscape in this century. "That was the start of a new kind of law," says one observer who was privy to the Court's biggest cases over decades. "No longer were people standing and taking two-handed set shots. No law is going to survive without being innovative and flexible."

Brown v. Board of Education (1954)

Those who watched remembered Earl Warren, "The Aircraft Carrier," posting up and calling for the ball four, five times in a row and kicking it back out until he saw a hairline crack in the defense or a teammate left completely undefended for a jump shot. "So agile for a big man," said one clerk. "They underestimated him at first, then they learned to play him tough. Not that it did them any good." (Interesting side note: Rumor has it that during oral arguments for the case, Warren was sizing up Thurgood Marshall, pleading for the appellants, and sent a page scurrying off to find out how tall he was.)

Griswold v. Connecticut (1964) {see fig. 2}

The case that made contraception safe for America was a nail-biter. Thirty-three years later, a man who watched the game while clerking for Hugo Black was still bitter as he recalled the improbable thirty-foot shot William O. Douglas made at the buzzer: "Two defenders hanging all over him, absolutely

FIG. 1. Pivotal play in *Hirabayashi v. United States* occurred with 1:23 left in the game, when Harlan Stone (1) dribbled to his left toward the top of the key (2) and then threw a behind-the-back bounce pass to Felix Frankfurter (3), who had faked outside and then cut back into the lane. Reed was busy trying to deny Rutledge the ball and so did not react in time to stop the pass.

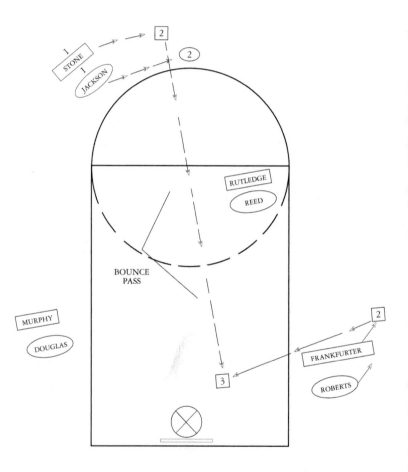

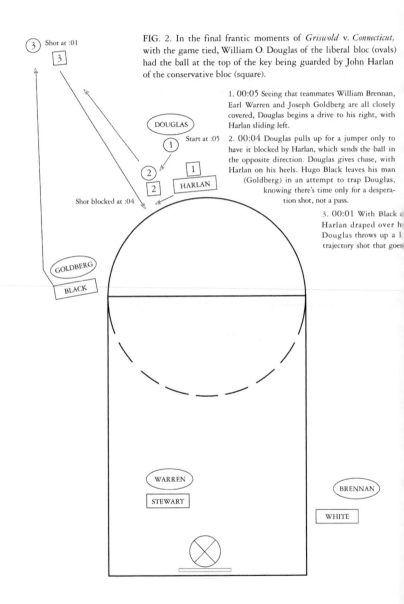

FIG. 2. In the final frantic moments of *Griswold* v. *Connecticut*, with the game tied, William O. Douglas of the liberal bloc (ovals) had the ball at the top of the key being guarded by John Harlan of the conservative bloc (square).

1. 00:05 Seeing that teammates William Brennan, Earl Warren and Joseph Goldberg are all closely covered, Douglas begins a drive to his right, with Harlan sliding left.

2. 00:04 Douglas pulls up for a jumper only to have it blocked by Harlan, which sends the ball in the opposite direction. Douglas gives chase, with Harlan on his heels. Hugo Black leaves his man (Goldberg) in an attempt to trap Douglas, knowing there's time only for a desperation shot, not a pass.

3. 00:01 With Black a
Harlan draped over h
Douglas throws up a l
trajectory shot that goes

Shot at :01

Start at :05

Shot blocked at :04

no arc, and it goes in—I mean, he should have apologized to everyone. But instead of acknowledging he was lucky, he goes and writes that crap about the 'penumbra of privacy' to rub our noses in it. What a prick."

Miranda v. Arizona (1966)
The case leading to the requirement that criminal suspects be informed of their rights. Warren again (fourteen points, nine rebounds, twenty-one assists), making it seem like there were eight players on his team instead of four. He also blocked out Stewart and defended Byron White so effectively that White threw the ball at Warren's head and drew a costly technical. The Court's legal historian put it in perspective: "Some justices—I'm thinking of Oliver Wendell Holmes here—had really high point totals, but their teammates suffered because of it. Earl made everyone else play better, and three men playing great is better than one any day."

New York Times v. United States (1971)
The "Pentagon Papers" game, in which Hugo Black and William O. Douglas, teammates for once, shared MVP honors. More than one clerk said that Black clearly was the game's outstanding player but that Douglas burned an indelible image into every brain with a monster dunk midway through the second half. "It got completely quiet for a few seconds, and then everyone—justices, clerks, refs—started to applaud. Then we had to wait another twenty minutes while they fixed the rim."

Furman v. Georgia (1972)
The death penalty game, when everything went to hell. Not only did several fistfights break out between sides, but justices were furious at their own teammates. After a while there was no passing; it got to be like a playground game where every person who grabbed a rebound turned and tried to take it himself to the other end. The result: a 16–16 final score, not even a pretense of choosing an MVP, and nine separate opinions. Bad

law all around, which was overturned just a few years later. A disgusted clerk who witnessed the game summed it up: "I don't care how many lives are at stake—you don't play like a bunch of municipal court thugs. A lot of my idealism died that day."

Roe v. Wade (1973)

"I've never seen someone take control of a game the way [Harry] Blackmun did that day," said one of his clerks. "He was on a mission. You could tell he had stopped being intimidated and had come into his own. He ran up and down the court for forty minutes, and after the first fifteen the conservatives were just holding their sides and wheezing. Nobody there was thinking about abortion or right-to-privacy—it was just, 'Look at Harry go!' "

Bakke v. California (1978)

Bakke wasn't the only one standing up to be heard; this was Lewis Powell's coming-out party as a player. He surprised everyone with his finesse, so fluid and graceful—almost courtly, in his Southern way, the way he ran the floor, dishing assists, getting everyone their points. But every time the defense collapsed on him and dared him to hit from outside, he arced shots that would melt in your mouth. Marshall was baiting him the entire game—understandable when you consider that the case threatened affirmative action—but Powell wouldn't bite, even after being elbowed again and again. Nobody remembers him hitting the rim the entire game.

Bowers v. Hardwick (1986)

Was a Georgia law against sodomy in violation of the Constitution? Perhaps more to the point, why couldn't Byron "Whizzer" White realize he didn't have it anymore as an athlete? His teammates voted him MVP to keep him happy, even though he was cherry-picking the entire game. Brennan, whom White was supposed to be guarding, was scoring from all over, but all Whizzer cared about was his own total. His teammates were banking on his hints that he was about to retire and thought giving him the honor would speed him out the door. It still took seven long years.

As you can see, the games have their own rich history, sometimes even overlapping with the Official Truth that made it into textbooks. Oliver Wendell Holmes actually did make the notorious statement, "Three generations of imbeciles are enough," but he was not, as widely believed, referring to the state-sanctioned sterilization of a retarded woman. He directed it at a referee, the grandson of an official whose incorrect interpretation of the rule book gave Chief Justice Roger Taney an extra throw in the Dred Scott horseshoe match. (The ref was a bit touchy about the whole subject; nobody wants to hear that their granddad prolonged slavery, so Holmes got tossed.) And, yes, Potter Stewart did say "I know it when I see it," but he was not talking about pornography, he was arguing with a ref about what constitutes traveling. The official did not accept his definition and responded, "Why don't you try playing defense and see how you like it?"

But enough about justices running their mouths. Let's focus on overall athletic skills. Since this is the first written account to make it to the public, a lot of inside info on earlier justices has died with the men who knew it firsthand. But with most former clerks of the past few decades ... still alive, it's possible to piece together fairly accurate descriptions of the recent ones. The consensus is that, as in the outside world, the modern players have it all over their counterparts from sixty years ago. It's a markedly different game. Dunks are so common now that no one bats an eye. It's also impossible to ignore the influence that steroids have had on the players. (Needless to say, Supreme Court justices do not submit to drug tests.) Strength and conditioning regimens allow the players to bring off athletic displays that were unimaginable in the thirties and forties.

FIG. 3. The **"S-T Zone"** (for "Scalia-Thomas") has been used effectively by moderates to force turnovers. With Scalia and Thomas inseparable, moderates can use one man (usually Kennedy) to defend them both, leaving an extra moderate player for double-teams. In this example, Rehnquist has the ball on top, guarded by Ginsburg and Breyer. When he passes to a fellow conservative, one of the two slides over to double-team the recipient, with the other defender staying put. Lately, Rehnquist and O'Connor have been able to negate the defensive scheme with back-door cuts. (Stevens: abstaining.)

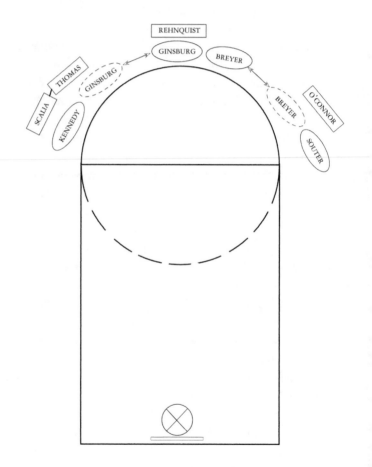

Still, steroids and conditioning only get you so far. As any sports fan knows, a lot depends on how well you play as a team and what you're willing to give after tip-off. After years of what they considered judicial overstepping by the Warren Court, conservative justices had high hopes for Warren Burger's boys. But when the games were on the line, the conservatives in the Burger Court just didn't want it as much.

Of course, they weren't helped by the fact that Burger was the worst player of all time. He was as bad as Ben Cardozo, but Cardozo could at least make free throws. Once, after Burger missed his eighth consecutive shot from the line, White gave him a withering look and said, "Thank you, Nixon."

Blackmun, though he had flashes of brilliance, was too often timid. White, of course, was still a formidable athlete when Kennedy appointed him, but he had lost a lot by the 1970s, even if he refused to admit it. (Marshall and Brennan constantly bickered over who got to guard him.)

The liberal holdovers from the Warren Court liked to torment the more conservative newcomers just to show who was boss. One example stands out in particular: It was said that Marshall, cantankerous in his final years, enjoyed taunting Scalia by mocking his fondness for hypothetical questions during oral argument. During one-on-one games that they played strictly for pride, every possession became an opportunity for Marshall to humiliate him: "What if one justice were to back in slowly—like this, say—dribbling the ball methodically, while his fellow justice stood there powerless to stop him? And what if the first justice then dunked over him, like … this?"

As for scouting reports on the current nine:

Chief Justice William Rehnquist: Bad back, hates to reach low for balls. Tends to turn it over if you force him to go to his left. Still, no one is able to see the whole court better. Opponents often think he's not even paying attention, and suddenly he's stolen the ball from them.

David Souter: Finesse player; doesn't like to bang. Moves

well without the ball; it's almost impossible to keep track of him. Drives defenders nuts and wears them out.

John Paul Stevens: Often wants to switch teams half-way through the game; it's hard to count on him in the late minutes.

Anthony Kennedy: Nondescript and workmanlike out there, but within the first week on the Court, he had memorized the dead spots on the floor and began forcing dribblers into them.

Sandra Day O'Connor: Got pushed around at first, but now uses her speed, and elbows. Runs the point well.

Antonin Scalia: Real trash talker. Constantly comparing himself to Warren, Black, and the other "maestros." Even the refs hate him.

Clarence Thomas: Was held in disdain by the other justices until his first game, when he let loose an eye-popping barrage of three-pointers. (The "Natural Law Fury from Above," as he called it.)

Ruth Bader Ginsburg: One of the best passers ever. Hooks up with Breyer in no-look alley-oops.

Stephen Breyer: Well-liked because he refuses to play dirty, even after taking cheap shots. Boxes out well.

Anyway, there you have the truth; it's up to you to handle it as best you can. And remember: I'll be judged by history. I don't know where the Court will go from here, now that the secret's out. Will they continue issuing opinions detailing how the votes broke down with faux precision? Will people be so outraged that political pressures will force—God forbid—an actual Supreme Court that tries to thrash out legal decisions based on logic?

The best we can hope is that everyone will submit to the higher power and let the shots fall where they may. Because at those critical moments when time stands still, as six of the justices clear out of the lane and one stands alone on top, dribbling the ball and eyeing the lone defender, this country reaches its full potential, a nation defined not by the past but by the moment. As the justice jukes and then brushes past his opponent and begins his rise to the goal, we all are lifted with him, knowing one thing at heart: If he can finish, so can we.

ACTUAL ACADEMIC JOURNALS WHICH COULD BE BROADWAY SHOWS IF THEY HAD EXCLAMATION POINTS ADDED!

T. G. Gibbon

Callaloo!

The Henry James Review!

Plainsong and Medieval Music!

The Lion and the Unicorn!

Modernism/Modernity!

RNA!

Organised Sound!

Field Mycologist!

Winterthur Portfolio!

ReCALL!

Continuity and Change!

The American Naturalist!

Wide Angle!

Radical History Review!

Modern Philology!

Popular Music!

Robotica!

Clinical Infectious Diseases!

The New Phytologist!

Yale Journal of Criticism!

Zygote!

MY BEARD, REVIEWED

Chris Bachelder

AVERAGE CUSTOMER RATING: *** (based on 9 reviews)

**** Must-see beard!!!
Reviewer: A. Dawson from San Antonio, TX, USA
This is the best beard I've seen all year. It's one of those beards
where you just never want it to end. If you get a chance,
CHECK OUT THIS BEARD. You won't be sorry. I guaran-
tee it.

** Disappointing
Reviewer: Monster Man from Baltimore, MD, USA
I see a lot of beards, and I usually really like first beards, so I
was excited about seeing Mr. Bachelder's beard, especially after
a friend of mine recommended it to me. But I'm sorry to say
that this beard was a big disappointment. You can see that it
has potential, but it's a little patchy and it just isn't doing anything new or interesting.

**** Not for everyone
Reviewer: Melissa T. from Eugene, OR, USA

This is one of those beards that not everyone is going to love, but I think it will find a cult following. It's a really funny and quirky beard. It's not completely full, but that almost makes it better somehow. Yes it's uneven and things get stuck in it, but it's a first beard, people! Congratulations, Mr. Bachelder, I can hardly wait for your next beard!!

***** AMAZING!!!
Reviewer: JD Vulture from Greenville, NC, USA

Oh my God this is an incredible beard!!! I saw a small part of Chris Bachelder's beard on the Internet and I just had to go see the whole thing. I was blown away. It's a hilarious beard, but it's also sad and touching. This girl beside me was crying because the beard was so emotional. I can't do it justice. Just do yourself a favor and see this beard. It's an instant classic, and I know you'll love it as much as I did.

* Don't believe the hype
Reviewer: Paul Russell from Lexington, KY, USA

I am baffled by the hype surrounding this beard. I decided to check the beard out after I read reviews calling it a "daring" beard, a "shockingly original" beard, "one of our best young beards." Some reviewers went so far as to compare it to Vonnegut's first beard. Well, nothing could be further from the truth. With Vonnegut, you never lose sight of the integrity and sincerity underlying the beard, but Bachelder's beard is just a tangled joke, and not even very funny, much less deep or substantive. Right now, the last thing this country needs is more smart-ass facial hair. At a time like this we need authentic beards. Bachelder's beard is the same beard we've been seeing for the last fifteen or twenty years, and it's getting old. Either do it right or shave.

*** Not great, not horrible
Reviewer: RW from Jacksonville, FL, USA
Let's not get carried away on either end. It's not a National Beard Award winner, but it's not trash, either. Bachelder's got a decent beard. It has a certain ragged charm, though I agree with others who have said it could have used a trim.

* Pathetic
Reviewer: Jennifer K. from Rochester, NY, USA
I just can't believe what passes for a good beard these days. I teach junior high English, and I've seen better beards on my eighth-graders. Don't waste your time. I'll take Hemingway's beard every time over today's beards.

**** A first look at an up-and-coming beard
Reviewer: Night Train from Silver City, CO, USA
Even though Mr. Bachelder won't let you touch his beard, his beard will touch you!! See it TODAY!!!!

**** Surprisingly deep
Reviewer: M-Dog from Tempe, AZ, USA
I was prepared to hate this beard after I found out about the huge advance that Bachelder got for it. And to be honest, I didn't think much of the beard when I first saw it, and I almost didn't finish looking at it. But I stuck with it and I'm glad I did. This beard has a way of sneaking up on you. Before I knew it, I was completely engrossed. It has a deceptively simple appearance, but this beard is actually very complicated and challenging. If you devote some time and careful attention to Bachelder's beard, it will pay you back, but you have to be willing to work.

THE NAME GAME

Stephany Aulenback and Sean Carman

TAKE THE NAME of your pet as your first name and the name of the street you grew up on as your last name. That's your Porn Star name.

Take the last name of the person you love as your last name. If you are a heterosexual woman, that's your Oppressed by the Patriarchy name. If you are a heterosexual man, that's your Sensitive New Age name. If you are a gay person of either gender, that's an affirmation of your love.

Take aim at your neighbor with a large club, then hit him over the head and take his wallet. Hide his body in the shrubbery outside his house. The name on his credit cards? That's your Fugitive from Justice name.

Take the kind of first name given to girls whose parents followed the Grateful Dead. Now take a patrician surname of English origin. That's your Public Defender's name.

Take a random six-digit number as your first name. Drop your last name. That's your official Prison name.

Take an interjection used to call attention as your first name. Take the proper term for a female dog as your last name. That's your unofficial Prison name.

Take the name you used back when everyone had C.B. radios. Boy, that takes you back, huh?

Take note of the name your cell mate whispers repeatedly in his sleep. That's your Stool Pigeon name.

Take the word "dead" as your first name, and a description of incest with your mother as your last name. That's your Marked by the Mafia name.

Take a name from the list of most common names for babies in 1965 as your first name. Take a name chosen at random from the phone book as your last name. That's your Witness Protection Program name.

Take your middle name as your first name. Take your mother's maiden name as your last name. That's your Romance Novelist name.

CIRCUMSTANCES UNDER WHICH I WOULD HAVE SEX WITH SOME OF MY FELLOW JURORS

Peter Ferland

JUROR #2. Malfunctioning elevator. We're late coming back from lunch, and the judge is going to be furious. The phone is dead and our shouts go unanswered. You're upset, so I calm you the only way I know how. Other than a desperate minute where I try to cough up the inhaled button from your shirt, it is a raw and sweet kind of lovemaking never before seen in the L.A. Criminal Courts Building. When they get the power back on, we're jolted back to our senses. We dress without a word and you disappear into the crowd. I watch the back of your head for the rest of the trial until we are dismissed with the thanks of the court. Thank you, I say aloud, but you don't turn around.

JUROR #4. Right there in the courtroom. The judge stops his instructions and calls attention to us, pointing out that there is a kind of feral chemistry between us, and does anyone else notice it? The bailiff confirms with a smile that heat radiates from the bench where we're sitting. The judge asks for a show of hands of people who object to postponing the work at hand to watch us get it on. There are no objections so, by order of the court, we embark on a rigorous and unselfconscious sexual workout that is one part ballet, one part Greco-Roman wrestling, one part Heimlich maneuver. The stenographer's record of the event is widely circulated.

JUROR #5. It has been eleven years of isolation after a desperate bailout over the Sahara desert. I have found shelter in a cave where I am haunted by recurring erotic dreams that last for hours but for some reason never result in a nocturnal emission. My hands were severed in the crash and it is impossible for me to masturbate. When the torment becomes too much for me to bear, I stagger out into the desert where I am sure I will die but instead I am found by your caravan where you feed and bathe me and tend to my wounds. You take me to your tent and onto your feather bed where, after lathering us both with scented lubricating oils, you invite me to take you. Still, I hesitate.

JUROR #6. You notice me.

JUROR #8. In the six days we've been here, a friendship was forged, right? We took lunches and played hearts together, shared *USA Today, People,* and *Reader's Digest.* I even loaned you my "Old Fart" hat because it was raining. But you and Juror Number 12 have started up a little thing, haven't you? Don't think I haven't noticed. You already had lunch and I should just go on ahead, right?—that's what you said. But then you and Number 12 went and had gyros. I saw you. Well, now Number 12 and the Alternate are playing charades in the stairwell and you're here in my room holding the pieces of your broken heart. Hush, now. I've got the glue, baby. I got the glue.

JUROR #9. This juror is me. It's after lunch and I have a few minutes to kill and the eye contact with the cafeteria money-taker has me all fired up. Or, I get stuck trying to make a left at that really long light on Sixth Avenue and the rhythmic thumping of the turn signal gets me hot. Or, it's been so long since I've done laundry that I have to choose between the leather thong underwear given to me as a joke from my secret Santa last year and wearing nothing at all under my conservative juror attire. (Come to think of it, it would be faster to list the circumstances under which I would not have sex with Juror Number 9: none.)

JUROR #11. We're on a hunting trip together. Even though I have no earthly interest at all in the following things: guns, woods, animals, you, I agreed to go because I'm proving to a former lover that I don't always reject things without trying them. On the third day, after doing what I can to ignore and deflect your ever-bolder sexual advances, I awaken to find you standing naked over me, deer rifle in hand, telling me there's an easy way and there's a hard way that this can go. And you voted to acquit! As is my custom in just about every situation that arises, I opt for the easy way. You're nervous and clumsy and I'd laugh if it weren't for the presence of firearms. When it's finally over, we have trouble making conversation. I welcome the bear attack.

THE BET

Arthur Bradford

I HAD MADE a bet with a guy named Fred about how many times I could punch him in the stomach before he threw up. He said that in point of fact, he would never throw up under such circumstances, but for the purposes of the bet, he gave me seven punches. That's a lot of punches, but Fred also knew that I don't possess a particularly powerful punch. Also included in the rules of the bet was the stipulation that Fred had to eat something substantial, like a sandwich, a few minutes before the punching began.

A lot of people were interested in the outcome of this bet. They wanted to watch. Either way it turned out, someone was going to be embarrassed. The winner, by the way, would receive a turkey, a nice one from a good supermarket. This seemed like the proper prize because this bet took place near Thanksgiving and many of us were planning on buying a turkey anyway.

I practiced punching a few times before the day of the bet. I punched a plastic jug of milk and it spilled all over the floor. Then I punched a cat that was walking across the counter. It said, "Yeow!" and jumped away. I hadn't really landed a good blow. I chased the cat through the house trying to get a good punch in, but whenever I got close enough, it ran away.

"Does anybody know whose cat this is?" I called out.

Nobody answered.

"I'm going to punch it!" I said.

I had the cat cornered in the back of one of the closets. I cocked my fist back and punched. The cat slipped away, as felines are wont to do, and my closed fist crashed against the wall. My knuckles immediately began to hurt and swell up.

"Oh fuck," I thought.

So I showed up to meet Fred the day of the bet with my good punching hand all swelled up and bruised.

"I was trying to punch a cat," I explained.

"Tough luck," said Fred.

We ordered up an oyster sandwich for him to eat. Then I was going to punch him in the stomach. Fred ate the sandwich slowly, slower than he usually ate, I thought. It seemed calculated to give him more time to digest. Everyone knows that the less time food has spent in the stomach, the easier it is to get it to come back up. It is this way with a lot of things. Like if you move in somewhere, the longer you are there, the harder it is to leave. Anyway, Fred took a half an hour to eat that oyster sandwich. Then he stood up and wiped his chin.

"Okay," he said, "punch me."

A pretty good crowd had gathered around for the bet. There were maybe twenty-five people watching to see what would happen. I didn't even know half of them. People started yelling things to me.

"Sock him good!"

"Give it to him!"

Now, as you should know if you've been reading this story carefully, my good hand wasn't usable at this point, so I had to wind up with my other hand and sock him with that. This wasn't a very effective course of action. That first punch proba-bly felt more like a gentle pat on the stomach to old Fred. The onlookers moaned and said things like, "Aw, geez...."

I stepped back and tried another punch, this one a little harder, more respectable. Still Fred didn't even seem close to barfing. He seemed pretty relaxed actually, like he found the whole thing to be a very simple challenge.

The crowd around us wasn't so calm. They couldn't believe what a wimpy puncher I was. I tried to explain to them:

"My good hand isn't working."

Still, they jeered.

"You wuss."

"Faggot."

I charged forward and socked Fred right in the crotch. This wasn't what I had meant to do, but due to the lack of coordina-tion in my other hand, it simply happened. My aim was low. I hit him pretty hard there too. Fred doubled over and the crowd began to cheer. Then something funny happened. Or I shouldn't say funny. I should say strange. Someone, a complete stranger from the crowd, jumped out at Fred and punched him in the face.

"Hey!" said Fred.

Then a woman leapt at him and started slapping his head and grabbing at his hair. A large hairy man with a ponytail stepped in and landed a good punch right in Fred's gut.

Fred fell to his knees and puked up the oyster sandwich. It splashed all over the floor and the crowd cheered.

Fred and I had to clean up the mess. Actually it was mostly me who cleaned it up because Fred was still hurting from the whupping he'd received. He was pretty upset.

"That was bullshit," he said.

"You owe me a turkey," I said.

"Fuck your damn turkey," said Fred.

He walked out of the bar. We were in a bar, by the way. I think I forgot to mention this earlier. It was the kind of bar that serves food. Most of the other patrons at the bar were drunk. This may explain why they turned on Fred the way they did. Perhaps it was the smug look on his face as I was punching him. I'm not sure, but I do know that I never got a turkey from him. And that doesn't surprise me at all. In fact, I bought him a turkey to show that I knew it wasn't fair what had happened. I brought it to his house a few days after Thanksgiving because I'm always late about bringing things over. Fred and his friends had already eaten plenty of turkey by then. Probably the last thing they wanted was another one, a little scrawny cheap one at that. I'd bought it at a discount. Fred opened the door and I realized what a dumb gift it was so I just threw it at him and walked away. You should have seen the look on his face when I did that. That was a funny look on his face just as the bony raw turkey body hit him in the chest. That was the last time either one of us made a bet like that, and by the way, my knuckles are all better now from that time when I hit the wall of the closet.

THE DANCE LESSON

Tim Carvell

1. Listen to the beat of the music.

2. Oh, for God's sake. Then turn some music on, will you? You were going to try to dance without any music playing? What's wrong with you?

3. I don't know. Something lively. Something with a beat to it. No, not that. Not that either. Fine, that'll do.

4. Okay, now listen to the beat of the music. Clap along to it. No, that's not it—you're going too fast. No, now you're going too slowly. That's it, you've got—no, you've lost it again.

5. How about this: Instead of clapping, just try to move your feet a bit to the music. Just shuffle them at a pace that seems right to you. Good, good, you've got it. That looks nice.

6. Let's take this up a notch now. Start moving your arms around to the music.

7. OH MY GOD. STOP MOVING YOUR ARMS THIS INSTANT. What was that? What were you doing? What the fuck was that supposed to be? I told you to move your arms, not flap them. You looked like a total dork.

8. First things first: When you move your arms, bend your elbows a bit. You don't have to hold them perfectly straight when you move them. Just bend your elbows a little. Bend them. You can bend your elbows, can't you? There.

9. No, you're not supposed to lock your elbows at a perfect right angle, either. You look like an organ grinder's monkey. Just relax a bit. Relax. RELAX!

10. So it's my fault that you can't relax? I don't think I've been "screaming at" you. I think I may have gotten a little agitated. I may have raised my voice a bit. But that doesn't constitute screaming.

11. Look, I'm sorry. I'm sorry. You're right. I was wrong, you were right. I know that teaching you to dance was my idea, and you've been a really good sport. I'm a jerk. I admit it. But I only yell at you because I want so badly to see you succeed—you know that. C'mon. Let's start over. Let's go back to where you were just shuffling your feet to the music.

12. Good, good, good. You're doing great. Just great. You look terrific. Now, let's try moving your arms a little to the music—just sway them back and forth a bit.

13. Um, OK, OK, that's … nice. That's really nice. But, you know, like I said before, you're allowed to bend your elbows just a bit.

14. That's super. Just super. You keep this up, and you'll be dancing great in no time. Now, try and vary your movements just a bit. Just go with the flow of the music. Improvise a little. You know, do what feels natural.

15. I'm sorry. I didn't mean to laugh. It's just that, when I told you to do what felt natural, I had no idea that what felt natural to you would be looking like … this.

16. Why are you crying? Oh, for Christ's sake, it's always like this with you, isn't it? I try and do something nice for you, and all of a sudden, you're all in tears because it hasn't turned out the way you planned. This is the thanks I get? Look: I'm trying to help you. I knew you'd have more fun if you knew how to dance, and so I agreed to take the time to teach you—time that I could have spent somewhere else, somewhere fun, hanging out with people who don't burst into tears for no reason. People who know how to take a fucking joke. I had other plans for today, but instead, here I am, being guilt-tripped by you for, like, the millionth time. You know I don't need this. You know I've got trust issues I've been working through. But don't let that stop you. No—you go right on ahead. Keep on crying, making me feel like a heel for trying to help you.

17. You're damn right, you're sorry.

18. Because I don't want to teach you, that's why.

19. Now you're going to dance? Without any input from me? Go ahead. Dance. I don't care.

20. I'm not watching you.

21. Okay, one quick pointer: You're still not bending your arms. Just a little. Just bend them a little. No, that's a jig. You're doing a jig. Oh, for God's sake….

ATTACK OF THE FABULONS!

Mark O'Donnell

(<u>OPEN ON</u>: THE VASTY DEEPS OF OUTER SPACE.
MUSIC: WEIRD THEREMIN SCI-FI.)

GENERAL
(VO, MAGNIFICENT)

A fragile thing, mankind. It survived the
savagery of the dinosaurs—by shrewdly
waiting until millions of years after their
extinction to evolve. It survived the Plague,
the Barbarians, and assorted great wars …
using methods you could probably go and
look up in a library. But nothing in mankind's
explosion-rich history prepared it for … the
Attack of the Fabulons!!

<u>SUPER</u>: TITLE "ATTACK OF THE FABULONS"

<u>MUSIC</u>: SCI-FI STING CHORD.

A FLYING SAUCER COMES INTO VIEW IN THIS STARSCAPE.

GENERAL (VO)
From the icy, glittering depths of space they came—icy and glittering themselves, and chic beyond imagining....

FADE TO: INTERIOR OF SAUCER. IT'S SPARE YET LUXURIOUS, HIGH-TECH SOHO. ISIDOR, ENSIGN, AND JANA WEAR BODY-FITTING SILVER SUITS AND SPORT BLOND *CHILDREN OF THE DAMNED* SALON CUTS. THEY ARE AS ICY AS THE PROFESSIONALLY FASHIONABLE CAN GET, EXCEPT ENSIGN, WHO HAS A TOUCH OF FEELING. JANA SCANS A PANEL.

JANA
We near the Earth, your fabulousness.

ISIDOR
Thank you, Jana. The earth. So light blue. Almost periwinkle. Light blue has such possibilities. As it is, though, Earth is just too cluttered. I see a makeover with lots of clean open spaces on it! Prepare the Destruct-o-Lasers.

JANA
Yes, Captain.

ENSIGN
Sir, some of their monuments are quite nice—

ISIDOR
Silence, Ensign! You are weak. Recite with me the Pledge of the Fabulons!

ALL
"To seek out and destroy all that is not in impeccable taste!"

ISIDOR DOES THE OBLIGATORY MAD LAUGH, THEN CHECKS HIMSELF.

> ISIDOR
> Ha ha ha ha! Excuse me. I bordered on kitsch there.

FADE TO: DARK LIMBO, OR MODEST PENTAGON WAR ROOM. GENERAL IS IN BEMEDALED GENERAL'S UNIFORM, AIDE HIS NEXT-IN-COMMAND. THEY TRACK THE SAUCER.

> AIDE
> What do you make of it, General?

> GENERAL
> It's like something from another world, Lieutenant!

> AIDE
> (DOESN'T TRY TO CORRECT HIM)
> Er—yes sir. Continue surveillance?

> GENERAL
> Yes. But don't anybody get trigger-happy here. These beings—or should I say entities— may be bringing us the cure for polio!

> AIDE
> We ... have the cure for polio, sir.

> GENERAL
> Dammit, you know what I mean! Let's keep a close monitor on them and see what their intentions are.

FADE TO: THE FLYING SAUCER IN EARTH'S ATMOSPHERE, OVER SOME TREETOPS.

CUT TO: STOCK FOOTAGE OR STILL PHOTO OF A STONE LAWN
JOCKEY.

GENERAL (VO)
They started small ...

ISIDOR (OS)
Focus laser! Fire!

SFX: SOUND OF KEEN LASER BEAM.
CUT TO: STOCK FOOTAGE OF MASSIVE EXPLOSION.
CUT TO: STILL PHOTO OR FOOTAGE OF THAT PINK HOT-DOG-
SHAPED SNACK HUT IN LOS ANGELES.

ISIDOR (OS)
Fire!

SFX: LASER BEAM.
CUT TO: STOCK FOOTAGE OF MASSIVE EXPLOSION.
CUT TO: PHOTO OR FOOTAGE OF EXTERIOR OF GRACELAND.

Fire! And hurry!!

SFX: LASER BEAM.
CUT TO: EXPLOSION AGAIN.
FADE TO: WAR ROOM AGAIN.

AIDE
We've just received word, General. The aliens
have destroyed Earth's last remaining Gabor
sister.

GENERAL
By God, they may yet go too far!

AIDE
Yet, sir?

GENERAL

Why these targets? It hardly seems strategic if
conquest is their mission here.

AIDE

Shall we fire on them, sir?

GENERAL

No, somehow I think that's what they want us
to do. And I don't want to fall into their trap.
Let's see their next move!

AIDE
(BEWILDERED)

Yes sir …

FADE TO: THE FLYING SAUCER FLYING OVER COUNTRYSIDE.

GENERAL (VO)

Insidiously, the Fabulons—though I didn't know their names at
the time—began to make their presence felt....

FADE TO: EXTERIOR SHOT OR FOOTAGE OF DISNEYLAND'S
SLEEPING BEAUTY CASTLE.

ISIDOR (OS)
Fire!

SFX: LASER BEAM.
CUT TO: STOCK FOOTAGE OF EXPLOSION.
CUT TO: EXTERIOR OF LAS VEGAS CASINOS.

ISIDOR (OS)
Jana, if you please!

SFX: LASER BEAM.

CUT TO: EXPLOSION AGAIN.

CUT TO: EXTERIOR SHOT OF TAJ MAHAL.

ISIDOR (OS)
No, leave that one.

FADE TO: INTERIOR OF FLYING SAUCER.

ENSIGN
Sir, you promised you'd leave the Eiffel Tower.

ISIDOR
I'm sorry, it was too labored, too clunky, like a
factory works.

ENSIGN
Is that bad? Industrial design can offer—

ISIDOR
I will not take aesthetic instructions from a
mere—

SFX: ODD RADIO SOUNDS.

JANA
Sir, we're being hailed on their armed forces
frequency.

ISIDOR
What do they want? Ohhh, give me that.

TAKES RADIO SPEAKER.

Fabulon Invasion Fleet. Design Director Isidor
speaking.

GENERAL (OS)
This is General Robert Rhubart of the
Pentagon.

ISIDOR
Oh yes, that wretched five-sided thing!

GENERAL (VO)
We must have a summit meeting to negotiate
an end to this destruction!

ISIDOR
You want a consultation, General? Don't you
like the work we're doing on your planet?

JANA
I hate it when clients want input.

ISIDOR
Ohh, very well, General. One o'clock. The
Calvin Klein showroom on Madison Avenue.
Oh, and General. One more condition.

GENERAL (OS)
Yes?

ISIDOR
Fresh-cut flowers in a *simple* vase.

FADE TO: EXTERIOR SHOT OF KLEIN SHOWROOM. A SIGN IN THE
WINDOW READS "SPECIAL SALE FOR ALIENS WITH VALID I.D."
FADE TO: INT. SHOWROOM. ACTUALLY, IT'S THE SAUCER
INTERIOR WITH THE EQUIPMENT REMOVED AND A MANNEQUIN
ADDED. THE ALIENS CONFRONT GENERAL AND AIDE.

ISIDOR
I like your uniform, General, though it's a
little busy.

JANA

On our world, men of your girth would be
destroyed.

GENERAL

Why this devastation?

ISIDOR

It's not devastation. It's redecoration. Soon
your planet will be as austere and streamlined
as this boutique.

PAUSE.

GENERAL

But ... don't you understand, though, that the
universe needs a cluttered, low-down planet
like Earth? There's plenty of cold planets. And
besides, high culture needs low culture to be
higher than!

MUSIC: FAINT INSPIRATION CHORDS.

We need the alpha and the omega, the micro
and the macro, hydrogen as well as uranium,
the zebra and the amoeba, Christian Science
and Christian LaCroix! And, you know
yourself, the stars themselves are overdone.

THE FABULONS ARE MOVED DESPITE THEMSELVES BY THIS
SPEECH, AND SNIFFLE HELPLESSLY.

ISIDOR

I never thought of it that way!

ENSIGN

Sir—you're crying!

ISIDOR
Yes, Ensign, I have been guilty of bathos. And
according to the Pledge of the Fabulons ...

ISIDOR, JANA, and ENSIGN
We must destroy ourselves!

ISIDOR POINTS A LASER GUN AT HIMSELF AND HIS STAFF.
CUT TO: ENORMOUS EXPLOSION FOOTAGE.
FADE TO: OUTER SPACE SWEEP AS SEEN AT TOP OF SCENE.

GENERAL
They never returned, not even to bill us.
Mankind went back to its sloppy, vulgar ways.
Earth. It may not be much ... but it's home.

FADE

PIRATE RIDDLES
FOR SOPHISTICATES

Kevin Shay

Q: What's a pirate's favorite aspect of computational linguistics?

A: PARRRsing sentences.

Q: Of which concept shared by Jungian psychology and Northrop Frye's literary theory are pirates especially fond?

A: ARRRchetype.

Q: Who's a pirate's favorite member of the creative team behind *32 Short Films About Glenn Gould*?

A: Don McKellARRR.

Q: Of all of Richard Harris's many achievements in the performing arts, which is a pirate's favorite?

A: "MacARRRthur PARRRk."

Q: What's a pirate's favorite alliance-creating diplomatic agreement from the Second World War?

A: The TripARRRtite Pact.

Q: Which ancient Greek lyric poet do pirates like the best?
A: PindARRR.

Q: If a pirate were to recite one of the Olympian odes by the aforementioned poet, which one would it be?
A: The XIth Nemean Ode, "To ARRRistagoras, the Prytanis of Tenedos, son of ARRRchesilaus."

Q: If that same pirate were then to recite a twentieth-century poem about the nature of poetry, what would it be?
A: "ARRRs Poetica" by ARRRchibald MacLeish.

Q: What if he went on to recite a poem by Sir Walter Scott?
A: "LochinvARRR."

Q: Why does that pirate keep reciting poetry, anyway? Is he some sort of nancy-boy?
A: Aye, 'tis a nancy-boy he be. Arrr.

Q: Of the ghosts that appear to Ebenezer Scrooge in *A Christmas Carol,* which do pirates prefer?
A: Jacob MARRRley.

Q: Can we replace that last one with something about Bob Marley, so we can have an additional gag about Rastaf-ARRRianism?
A: No.

Q: Whom did the pirate vote for in the Haitian election?
A: ARRRistide.

Q: Wait. Why did they let a pirate vote in the Haitian election?
A: Remember, the nation was taking its first halting steps

toward democracy, and balloting procedures were rather chaotic. The pirate just slipped in somehow. Arrr.

Q: I don't buy it. Pirates care nothing for participating in the electoral process.
A: Look, can we finish this up soon? I'm having those phantom pains in my wooden leg.

Q: A phenomenon first described in the seventeenth century by which important contributor to the field of amputation surgery?
A: Oh, this is getting ridiculous.

Q: Just say it.
A: Ambroise PARRRé.

Q: You can go now.
A: Arrr. Nancy-boy.

A SHORT FICTIONAL PASSAGE ENTITLED "DRIFT NETS," IN WHICH SEVERAL ENTERPRISING CHARACTERS TROLL THE HIGH SEAS, EXPLORING ABANDONED TRADE VESSELS FOR "PIRATED" GOODS, AND LEARN TO COPE WITH DISTINCT PERSONALITIES IN A CLOSE-KNIT, HIGH-STRESS ENVIRONMENT

Todd Pruzan

As SOON AS they hoisted him back over the railing, onto the deck—before they could even see his face—they knew Philip Glass had hit the jackpot. He'd surfaced with a thumb up, and crooked in the other arm of his rubber suit he had two dark green bottles and a small trunk. They'd lifted Philip Glass carefully from the water to avoid dropping his find back into the sea.

Now his helmet was off, and Philip Glass was whooping.[1]

---

1. The principles of comedy, of delivering humor to an audience, hold that the first joke may not get a predictable response. This story's readers are still trying to find their footing in the story, to gauge whether they can determine the author's wavelength and follow it. The first citation of the name "Philip Glass" will undoubtedly remind some readers of the avant-garde composer who shares the character's name; the first repetition of the name may even induce a chuckle, as the disparity between the nature of the character and the nature of the composer would seem to be tremendous indeed. But by the third citation of his name, in which the character is actually "whooping," readers may be greatly amused by the connection of the name Philip Glass with an activity that seems out of character for the Philip Glass they know from real life.

"Four hundred years on the ocean floor!" The crew was grinning as they helped him out of his diving suit. Stephen Glass[2] gently plucked the chest from Philip Glass's arm and set it on the deck. It was heavy. Heavy was good. Although they all knew it could be full of sand, in this case they all shared the same feeling—this was the real thing. Stephen Glass was hoping they'd let him jimmy it open with his Swiss Army knife.

When they got it open, it was something to behold.

"Wow. Four-hundred-year-old rum," said Stephen Glass.

"Pretty incredible, isn't it," said Philip Glass. "They made bottles pretty different back then. You drop that on the deck, it'll break into big chunks."

Stephen Glass put the bottles down gently.

"You should take a dive yourself, Stephen. The fish down there are pretty spectacular too."

"Actually, I'd rather stay here and get a taste of that rum," said Stephen Glass.

"Shut the fuck up," said Ira Glass.[3]

He'd been hearing about the rum for a fortnight now, knot after knot, and he was at the end of his rope. Ira Glass had had

---

2. The repetition of the name Glass is becoming apparent by now, but the name Stephen Glass may also earn laughter from any reader familiar with the career of the disgraced former journalist. Some readers may pay particular attention, envisioning some sort of poetic revenge—but again, such anticipation may be a result of projecting an expectation of the scandalized, real-life Stephen Glass onto this character who shares his name.

3. By the third appearance of the surname Glass, the author's joke is fully clear to almost every reader, and an audience laughs as one. But the joke here is twofold: Not only is there humor in the unlikelihood of an expedition team comprised entirely of people named Glass, but the name Ira Glass itself would appear not to fit such a crude expletive as that to which this character is attributed. Many readers will recognize the name Ira Glass from a weekly syndicated public radio program called *This American Life,* and its host's gentle, endearing, friendly voice and manner stand in stark opposition to the cruelly banal rejoinder offered here. Therefore, humor arises also from the shock of the situation, not merely from the now-predictable repetition.

passengers like Stephen Glass before, but usually his impressive bulk and salty language were enough to put off anyone's complaints. Creeping alcoholism, however, was another matter. He'd dealt with it in his crew, but never in so brazen a paying customer.

"We're going to lock that chest away," Ira Glass said, "and we're going to have Seymour take a look at it when we return to port. And that's the end of it. Now who's ready for a dive?"

Seymour Glass[4] was ready, but he'd been down once that morning and had seen enough for one day. He'd come up short—a broken empty flask. Complete trash. Worth less than sand. "I'm OK, thanks," he said.

"Can I take a peek?" said George Glass.[5]

"Yeah, let's get you fitted with that helmet," Ira Glass said, taking it from the bench next to Philip Glass's right foot.

He was almost suited up when they heard a loud curse from the cabin. "What is it?" Ira Glass shouted.

Bill Blass[6] appeared in the doorway, his face dark. "There's a hurricane on the way, boys." The deck fell silent.

---

4. By this point, the central joke of this passage—the repetition of the name Glass, and the naming of characters after well-known, unaffiliated bearers of the surname—is abundantly clear, and any laughter that appears here is a diminishing return on the author's investment. Such laughter will be polite and subdued; the author now must heighten the tension with a surprising joke, which, paradoxically, the audience has come by now to subconsciously expect.

5. Here, the payoff is tremendous. George Glass is a memorable name that appeared in an episode of the TV series *The Brady Bunch*—an anti-intellectual response to the preceding names of an avant-garde composer, a fallen journalist, a public-radio host, and a character from fiction by J. D. Salinger. The twist in tone—from high culture to banality—is a satisfying one. It could, conceivably, serve as the passage's last "joke." Any other attempted jokes must be handled deftly to keep from capsizing the heightened mood of the audience.

6. A wonderful denouement. The twist in the "name game"—from Glass to, suddenly, Blass—would throw any audience member off the scent. The idea of fashion designer Bill Blass serving as a yachting expedition's first mate is also incidentally hilarious, and the double-joke here is enormously gratifying.

INEFFECTIVE LINES DELETED FROM FINAL REVISIONS OF VIOLENT BOX-OFFICE HITS

Dan Kennedy

—Why don't you get a sugar packet or a little piece of napkin and put it under the table so it doesn't wobble. Because when I shoot you, you're gonna need a nice firm surface to collapse onto.

—Do yourself a favor: Clean off the letters and papers from your desk and get it organized. Put the bills on one side and the junk mail in the trash. I want it to look real nice and orderly when they find your body here.

—Wash your car. Wash it real good, but if I were you I wouldn't waste your time applying a coat of wax … because by the time it dries and is ready to be buffed off of there, you'll be dead.

—You a big tough guy? If you're so tough why don't you stick your head up your ass and join the army. Why don't you spit on the ground and I'll swim in it or whatever. Huh? [Pulls back hammer on gun.]

A GRACELAND FOR ADOLF
Zev Borow

> The State of Bavaria said today that it had found an investor to turn the site of Hitler's 262-acre retreat at Berchtesgaden, his official summer residence near the Austrian border, into a tourist attraction.
>
> —*New York Times*

Selections from the audiotape accompanying the walking tour of "Berchtesgaden: Hitler's Summer Retreat":

"WELCOME TO BERCHTESGADEN, Hitler's fabulous place in the country. Naturally, the Führer had his own special nickname for his beloved retreat, an Austrian folk expression that translates roughly to: "All the small birds are dead now." Yes, Hitler loved folk expressions. And hated birds. [*Pause*] Stand straight! [*Pause*] The Führer would arrive here at the start of summer weekends, exhausted from tyranny and evil. Close your eyes and imagine how it must have been then, without the adjacent petting zoo. Hitler would arrive, gaze at his sur-roundings, and likely feel the beginnings of a smile, perhaps the first to creep across his cherubic face all week. For here, all the small birds were dead, exterminated actually, in 1938. Open your eyes now, and, at your own pace, walk ahead....

"The front door. Now, we'll have to ask all Jews, Catholics, and Macedonians to wait out front while the tour continues inside.... Just kidding—all are welcome! Step in and see the wonders of this palatial home. Move along....

"Growl if you like sauerbraten! Welcome to the Jungle ... Room. And you thought only Elvis liked panther skin! This positively wild place is where Hitler would entertain some of the most fabulous Nazis in the world with lots of alcohol and late-night 'winner-take-all' Scrabble. Notice the custom-made swastika-shaped waterbed and accompanying shag rug. And dig that groovy mural! Walk ahead. Eyes forward.

"Hitler loved to surround himself with pretty things, and vari-ous kinds of poisons, especially here in his bedroom. The flower-print bedspread and matching snapdragon wallpaper are the perfect complement to Hitler's collection of hand-carved cat figurines. The shelves toward the back bay window—the Führer made those curtains himself!—hold a dizzying collec-tion of flavor-infused arsenics. Truly, a room where both Laura Ashley and a trained assassin hired to kill Laura Ashley would feel right at home. Now, march.

"Hitler's study, a refuge from his topsy-turvy world, where he could jot down any little thought that popped into his head—say, a haiku to his dead mother, a nifty Polish joke, notes on an idea for a screenplay about cops gone bad, or just a doodle of his imaginary friend, Sandy, who Hitler believed lived in the attic and came up with the strategy for invading Russia.

"When Hitler was stressed, more often than not this was where you could find him, in Berchtesgaden's gym. He'd spend hours here, practicing karate with his bodyguards, screaming into a full-length mirror, enduring marathon Taebo workouts, whatever. Yes, Hitler was extremely flexible. Why not let one of our armed guards twist you into a pretzel? Ha!

"The yard. Nothing relaxed the Führer more than being astride a rideable lawnmower. An early proponent of organic fertilizers and home mulching, Hitler cared deeply about green, healthy lawns. In fact, Hitler once said that if he had another life to live, he would still try to conquer the world for the Aryan race, but first he'd conquer the menace that are dandelions and nasty weeds. Achtung! Time to go....

"Sure, Hitler loved human suffering, but he also liked music—for marching, for dancing, for making one feel less sexually inferior. Music. And this was his music room. Look, behind the vintage Moog synthesizer is Hitler's old accordion. That's right, as a teenager the Führer was in a rock band, albeit one that included an accordion player. The group, named Torchyr, after a joke Hitler's uncle used to tell, actually grew quite renowned in the clubs of Munich with songs girded by knowing pop structure and meticulously crafted harmonies.

"Hitler's garage. Here's where the Führer would pore over ball bearings for his still-unfinished collection of kit '30s Fords, sniff turpentine, or just fiddle at his workbench. That old-fashioned loom—Hitler loved to loom—in the corner has the tooth marks of a madman, and behind that are some really sharp knives. Indeed, here in the garage one can't help but get a sense of just how creative a man Hitler really was, and, while at Berchtesgaden at least, how happy and at ease. [*Pause*] This concludes our tour. Thanks once again for coming. Peace."

TRINITY

Neal Pollack

PART ONE

PORTRAIT OF AN ANDALUSIAN
HORSE TRAINER

AT SEVEN A.M. on a recent Tuesday, Paolo Luciamonte, the last great Andalusian horse trainer, arose from bed, spat on the floor, and put a fresh pot of coffee on the stove. As the fog of sleep evaporated from Paolo's brain, he stared out his kitchen window into the crisp Andalusian dawn, like he'd done every morning for the last twenty-seven years. The colt loomed monstrously in front of the swirling clouds. El Caballo de Sangre. The Horse of Blood. The death horse. The greatest challenge Paolo Luciamonte had ever faced.

"Today is the day I will break the spirit of the Horse of Blood," Paolo muttered into his cup of steaming brew. "Today he will learn. No horse is useful unless he can be ridden for money. No horse is free in my stable."

I had come to Andalusia as a reporter, to learn what it was

157

like for a man who had never known any other way of life to train horses in a world that had increasingly less use for his services. As I'd driven the previous night down the highway from the Barcelona airport toward Rancho Luciamonte, listening to Madonna's *Ray of Light* CD on my Discman, I thought about my grandfather, T. Burlington Glass III, who had trained horses himself at our family ranch in Texas while I was growing up. I marveled at what a different person I turned out to be from my grandfather, the world's largest manufacturer of tube socks and low-grade nuclear weapons, me a freelance magazine writer, published novelist, founder of an experimental kindergarten in the Bronx, and male fashion model. I wondered why my life had turned out so differently from his.

Then I realized: horses. My grandfather and grandmother, with whom I spent every summer when I wasn't on the island of Corfu with my parents, Jackie Onassis, and Andy Warhol, were obsessed with horses. When they weren't riding them, they were breeding them. When they weren't breeding them, they were racing them. Horses spurred my grandparents to great passions.

I loved horses then as well, and pranced them relentlessly until that one day Grandpa made me take a special ride.

My grandparents retained the services of a Nubian manservant named Carlos, who was a pretty big guy, nearly twice my adult size—and I've been told by numerous award-winning actresses whom I've dated that I have a nice body. One day, as Grandpa and I were counting my inheritance money in front of a roaring fire, he called Carlos into the room.

"Carlos," he said, "it's time to play horsey."

Although Carlos protested slightly, soon Grandpa had him whinnying on his hands and knees. He then placed me astride his houseboy's broad, firm back, thrust a whip into my hand, and said: "Don't just sit there, boy, make Carlos giddyap!"

"But—" I protested.

"Don't worry," said Grandpa. "Carlos likes being a horsey, don't you, Carlos?"

Carlos, who had a stainless-steel bit jammed firmly between his teeth, could not respond. Grandpa thrust a pointy boot into his rear, and he began to move. As I trotted Carlos around the room, I asked Grandpa why he was making me do this hideous, slave-driving thing.

"Boy," Grandpa said, "there are two kinds of men in life: trainers and horses! And for a Newsworthy, every other man is a horse, black or white! Remember that! Don't ever let another man saddle you up and get you into a lather!"

"Whoa, Carlos!" I shouted. "Whoa!"

I dismounted the debased Nubian and turned to my grandfather. "I don't want your stinking golden bridle!" I shouted. "I'm gonna make my own way in the world!"

I ran out of the ranch, down the mile-long driveway, and onto the county road, sobbing and cursing the day I was born a Glass. I was seventeen years old and already a Harvard graduate, but what did that mean when I had a super-rich racist grandpa?

Now here I was, in Andalusia, watching Paolo Luciamonte, the last of the great Andalusian horse trainers, get tossed around like Raggedy Andy by El Caballo de Sangre. The Horse of Blood.

"This was to be my day of greatest triumph," he said to me. "But instead, I have just ruined another pair of blue jeans. I cannot defeat this horse. This is the last great horse in the world. No man can tame El Caballo de Sangre. The Horse of Blood. It cannot be done."

The Horse of Blood snorted in defiance. Paolo sighed.

"I will turn you into mere sausage," he said. "Someday. Someday."

"Paolo," I said. "May I try riding El Caballo de Sangre? The Horse of Blood?"

"Great Journalist from Brooklyn, you will surely be killed!" Paolo said in heavily accented English. "I, the greatest horse trainer in Andalusia, mount him every day, and he's turned my nuts into butter! What chance do you stand?"

"Let me attempt this feat," I said. "It's for the good of my story, which I am writing for an important magazine with a large circulation."

Paolo sighed bitterly, and turned away. He could not stand to witness my fate, and also could not understand that this was an act into which destiny had forced me. I had come to Andalusia to write a story about Paolo, but my mission had suddenly been obscured by the darkness of memory. The tragic last years of a centuries-old way of life are nothing compared to my wine-dark soul's screaming need for redemption.

As Paolo watched from the house, the sun began its sad descent below the great horizon of the grassy plain. I mounted El Caballo de Sangre, the Horse of Blood, and dug man-made stirrups into his flesh with my powerful spurs.

"This one's for you, Carlos," I grunted, and rode the son of a bitch into the dirt.

PART TWO
THIS ALBANIAN LIFE

I'VE BEEN GOING to bed lately on a pile of jagged stones covered only by a thin cotton blanket half-eaten by moths. This is one of the worst possible sleeping arrangements I could imagine. Sometimes I wonder how things got this way. I have to remember that I am a twenty-six-year-old journalist, novelist, radio producer, and poet, and I am here in Albania to find out what life is really like for a family in the poorest country in Europe. I have personally borne witness to much human suffering and am here to tell you: Things are not good.

We had dirt for lunch today. All twenty-three of us. Jumanji, the patriarch of the family, is a short, bald, armless man who looks older than his eighty-seven years. He tells me that dirt has been in short supply in Albania lately, and he worries about the health of his family. I tried to make our lunch taste better using some of the skills I had learned at the

Culinary Institute of America. It didn't help much. Here I was, a former Rhodes scholar, and what did it all matter, really?

Although this family's house has no plumbing, consistent heat source, or exterior walls, they do have satellite TV. I was tired today from all my reporting, so I watched a lot of CNN. I saw that a good friend of mine had won a jury prize at the Sundance Film Festival. I think about all the awards and honors I've won in my life, the trophies and ribbons, but in the face of all this Albanian poverty and hopelessness, they seem somehow meaningless now. You know what I mean?

I wake up early this morning and watch the village children play soccer with the bloated carcass of a cat. I've been here so long that this kind of thing doesn't bother me anymore, so I join in. I score three goals and make a game-winning save. The children all gather around me and want to know about my life in the more bohemian sections of Brooklyn. I show them a picture of my girlfriend. "She is very beautiful," says one of them. "Yes," I say, "and very wealthy. She is a human rights activist who has also written three prize-winning novels." Later, a man is impaled on a stake in the town square. I want to ask: For what crime? But I do not speak Albanian.

I am leaving tomorrow. The town has pooled its remaining money together, three dollars, to throw me a farewell party. I hug Grandma Ninotchka, my favorite family member, for a long time. She works twenty hours a day, six days a week, as a plutonium miner to feed her family. And spends her precious free time, what little there is, as a volunteer grave digger. "You have brought a beacon of hope into our terrible, terrible lives," she says. "And God bless you for not stealing my oatmeal like the man from the *New York Times*."

I am not prepared for the immense wave of emotion that I am experiencing. Nothing I went through in college, not even having dinner with two presidents, could have possibly prepared me for this. I cry silent tears, and pray for the people of this sorrow-ridden country, and for myself.

PART THREE
I HAVE SLEPT WITH 500 WOMEN

PERHAPS YOU THINK that it would be easy for me, an Ivy League graduate and published novelist who has a good-paying day job at a major television network, to find true love. But it is not. I have searched everywhere—Chicago, San Francisco, Seattle, Paris, Rome, and even, on occasion, Brooklyn—for the woman who would be the ideal match for my unique mix of intelligence and mild but endearing neuroticism.

Nothing has emerged. I have found no love. No one with whom to share my life.

Instead, all I have found is sex, and nothing but. I have slept with 500 women, maybe more, but certainly not fewer. No matter where I go, no matter what the occasion, I always end up having sexual intercourse with some woman. They are usually beautiful, intelligent, charming, and sophisticated. They generally think I'm pretty hot. We often delight in the curves of each other's bodies. We always fuck like wildebeest.

But we never fall in love.

Just last night, for instance, I was at a party thrown by the chief editor at a major publishing house, who happens to be a good friend of mine. I hadn't been there five minutes when I fell into conversation with a sleek, black-haired beauty, a prize-winning poet and ranking business executive who is also the director of a folkloric music festival in her native country of Peru. Sure enough, within an hour, we were fuckin'!

This morning, I turned to her and said, "Do you think we could ever fall in love with each other?"

"Love is for fools," she said. "Ram me again, you hot stud! Ram me all day long!"

My diet of unhindered sexual pleasure grows less nourishing every day. Sometimes, I am plunged into depressions that cannot be cured, not even by massive doses of St. John's wort. When I'm on assignment in, say, northern Spain, and the women of Barcelona are launching themselves at me like rockets, I want to scream, "Por favor! Leave me alone!" But I don't, and soon enough I'm trapped once again in the pit of knives that more naive men call "the sack." At times, only the slim, ephemeral dream that I will someday fall in love keeps me from shuffling off this wretched, tormented, sex-filled mortal coil.

I am tired of being propositioned on airplanes. I cannot tell you how many times I've been forced into illicit sex in public toilets. One grows tired of having an opera singer grinding on one's face while a conceptual artist sucks mightily between one's legs. It loses its charm.

Enough of sex! Enough fellatio! Do you hear me, women (and men) of the world! I don't want to fuck you anymore! I only want your love. Love me, dammit, love me! Love, love, love! People of the world, hear my cry! I am your hobbyhorse no more!

POP QUIZ
Sean Condon

"Who's That Girl?" Madonna
I'm not sure. Is it Rosanna Arquette? Or one of her sisters? It kind of looks like Rosanna, but why would she be hanging out here?

"Who Let the Dogs Out?" Baha Men
That little bastard Timmy from next door. But what can you expect with parents like his? I think the father spent some time in Attica or Raiford or somewhere like that.

"Who's That Girl?" Eurythmics
I think it's Rosanna Arquette. Or Patricia. Is there another Arquette sister because if there is maybe it's her.

"Why Do Fools Fall in Love?" Frankie Lymon and the Teenagers
Well, it's easier for them than us intellectuals. They have lower standards about pretty much everything. Food, lovers, ciga-

rettes, everything. I pity fools, I really do. Hey, did I sound like Mr. T just then?

"Where Have All the Flowers Gone?" Pete Seeger
They were taken by truck at dawn to a wholesale market and sold at inflated prices to retailers who will in turn sell them at inflated prices to people like you and me. That's pure capitalism, my friend, pure capitalism.

"What's It All About, Alfie?" Dionne Warwick
It's about growing up and trying to face your emotional responsibilities. That and chasing trim.

"If I Said You Had a Beautiful Body, Would You Hold It Against Me?" Bellamy Brothers
If I told you that while I do indeed have lovely contours the skin on my back is quite horribly scarred, would you still want me to hold my beautiful body against you? Unless you meant would I resent you for giving me a compliment, then I apologize and just forget that stuff about the scars.

"What Are You Doing Sunday?" Tony Orlando
Church. If I don't have a hangover. But I'll probably have a hangover.

"Will You Be Staying After Sunday?" Peppermint Rainbow
If I don't go to church or have a hangover, I'm getting the first bus back to the city. Your parents are driving me fucking nuts. But I'll probably have a hangover.

"How Is Julie?" The Lettermen
She's well. She got that job at Morgan Stanley she was hoping for, and she and Jim have set a date, finally, and everything seems to be going really well for both of them. Although just between you and me, I think Jim's still tomcatting with his

secretary. Don't tell Julie, though, it'd kill her. Oh, I almost forgot, she said to say hi.

"Why Didn't Rosemary?" Deep Purple
Why didn't she what? What sort of a question is that?

"Do You Love As Good As You Look?" Bellamy Brothers
You again?

"What Will Mary Say?" Johnny Mathis
We'll break it to her gently, and hopefully she'll be mature about it. But my guess is she'll scream something along the lines of, "You bastards, how could you?" You know her weakness for clichés when she's hysterical. God, this is gonna be awful. Let's tell her tomorrow.

"Why? Why? Why?" Ray Smith
Ray, Ray, Ray—do we have to keep going over this? If I've told you once, I've told you a thousand times. Because. And this has nothing to do with me and Johnny and Mary, by the way, so don't get all paranoid.

"Why Can't I Be You?" The Cure
Well, the position's filled. Besides, you're very good at being you. Not many guys can get away with lipstick the way you do.

"What Have I Done to Deserve This?" Pet Shop Boys & Dusty Springfield
You denied your sexuality for too long, Dusty.

"Can I Touch You ... There?" Michael Bolton
Not as long as you ... keep on releasing albums like *My Secret Passion: The Arias.* And that haircut you used to have is still kind of hard to forgive. So the answer's no.

"Who Are You?" The Who
Do you want to know my name? Or, like, who I *really* am?

"Are You Experienced?" Jimi Hendrix
Not in the area you specifically require, but I'm a fast learner. I know people say that about themselves all the time, but I really am. Really.

"How Do You Talk to an Angel?" Heights
Very slowly. Most of them are kind of stupid.

"Who Can It Be Now?" Men at Work
Probably the UPS guy. They said they'd be here between noon and six. What's it now—around four?

"Are You Lonesome Tonight?" Elvis Presley
I'm lonely most nights, Elvis. I just can't seem to make friends here. I shouldn't have left Ingrid back in Plaistow but, God, her parents were really driving me crazy. I hit the bottle pretty hard for a while because it was the only way I could stand to be around them. It's just so difficult to meet people—*normal* people—in this city. Most nights I just sit at home watching TV or thinking about stuff. Sometimes I call a friend back in Plaistow and see what's up.

"Do You Know the Way to San Jose?" Burt Bacharach
Yes.

"Where Did It All Go Wrong?" Oasis
I'd say almost immediately after "(What's the Story) Morning Glory?" That's an obvious answer, and quite glib, I realize, but it's true. Boy, is it true.

"Will You Marry Me?" Paula Abdul

Well, I probably would if it wasn't for the fact that you were once married to Emilio Estevez and I just can't stand that guy. I'd be thinking about you and him all the time.

"Would I Lie to You?" Eurythmics

Well you've lied to me on numerous occasions before, so I wouldn't be surprised. That bullshit about Rosanna Arquette being at the club that night with you and Madonna was just bullshit, and that's a perfect example of the way you lie to me. Probably to everyone.

BAD NAMES FOR PROFESSIONAL WRESTLERS

Jeff Johnson

Linus

The Spiller

Lace

The Soup-Eater

Stilts

The Tailor

Mitochondria

Kimono Boy

The Really Tiny Moth

The Bulimic Cheerleader

Winston Churchill

Vasco da Gama, Jr.

Tickles

The Fig Wasp

Cookies 'n' Creme
    [tag-team duo]

The Healer

El Wusso

The Precocious Feline

The Professor

Balsamic Vinegar

The Stooge

Diabetes

Warren G. Harding

The Wilting Zinnia

The Schoolboy

The Yearling

The Pediatrician

The Old Coward

Naomi

The Narcoleptic

Magic Realism

EVIDENTLY, IT WAS LIVE THEN

Dan Kennedy

Sal Salbert (host, producer):
Oh, it was nuts. You think this stuff today is funny? You think the nighttime comedy programs these days are funny? [I start to answer, but he keeps talking.] We literally invented comedy television. We had one sketch back then that we did called "The Silly Italian," and what I would do was come out on stage in an Italian costume, with the hair and all, holding a jug of wine and saying, "Mama mia ... maaa maaa mia...." The crowd just howled. They loved it! Then what I would do is I would wait a minute for them to stop laughing, and then I'd give them a long one. You'd see me waiting. You could always see it in my eyes. Carl used to watch me from the wings, and he knew it was coming. I'd get that look in my eyes and then I'd give them a real good long, "Maaaaaaaaaaaa ... maaaaaaaaaaaaaaaaaaaaaaaa ... miiiiiiaaaaaaaaaaaaaaaaaaaaaaaaaaaaaaa!" And it was live back then! No videotape! No computers! No editing, nothing! So if you screwed up your line, well ...

[shrugs and makes a "tough luck for you, buddy" face, because it was live].

*   *   *

Carl "The Doctor" Negel (head writer, 1950–1954):
My toes were always stubbed from kicking the wall in the writers' room. I kicked it every time somebody forgot a line I had written. Everybody remembers the sketch called "The Silly Italian," and when they recall it they always say, "Oh, yeah ... that was the Mama Mia guy." Well, there were a dozen other lines Silly Italian was supposed to say, but half of the time all Sal remembered to say was the one line. So every time he didn't say, "Bella! Marinara spicy meatball!" or "Who got a pizza on my stromboli!" I kicked that damn wall. But those were the days.... We were the ones who came up with what your generation recognizes as TV comedy, but the difference was, when we were doing it we had one take to do it in. It was all live back then, so if the actors missed the line ... that was it. No rewinding it to make it better. You couldn't go crying to some director with a robotic camera like today. This was live TV, my friend.

[I ask what a robotic camera is.]

[Silence.]

[I mention that *Saturday Night Live* is also a live program.]

[Carl asks Sal why I'm a wiseguy, and they start repeating whatever I say, except in a high-pitched voice. As they do this, they're cracking up, and me, I'm not laughing.]

*   *   *

Nan Breckenridge (writer, performer 1950–1952):
Oh, I don't remember too, too much about the material back

then, but it seemed like we had a good time and made a little money. That was more than I had intended to do, so you could say the show was a success.

[I politely ask her not to be so modest.]

Oh, I don't know that I'm being modest. I just think that we did our job and that was that.

[I tell her that Carl and Sal claim it was quite a lot more than that.]

Oh, Sal this and Carl that. I distinctly remember thinking, "What is so brilliant about 'The Silly Italian'? It's base." That sketch was really the beginning of the end for me on that show.

[I tell her how Carl and Sal made fun of me when I mentioned that *Saturday Night Live* was also a live program.]

Well, Sal thinks he's the only comic to ever work live. I mean, if Sal says hello to you at Hamburger Hamlet on a Tuesday, he spends all day Wednesday and Thursday pointing out that it was live when he said hello to you and that if he had blown it, there would have been no editing that could save him from having said hello incorrectly. The live thing always gets me, because what line was Sal going to louse up so badly without the "safety net" of editing? "Mama mia?"

[She and I are both laughing at that one. I like Nan. Through our laughter, I add in a little comment about how when Sal and Carl were making fun of me it wasn't even that funny. I say, "They could've come up with something better than just repeating everything I said in a girlish voice."]

[I finish laughing, but Nan is laughing even harder now.]

Oh, actually … that's pretty funny because you do have that high-pitched voice, hon. You … [laughing] do almost … sound like … [laughing harder] I mean, don't take it the wrong way but … [wiping her eyes, still laughing] Oh, my …

[Pulls herself together and behaves like a grown adult for a moment.]

After I talked to you on the phone, I called Sal and asked him if the nice lady from the magazine had called them about doing an interview, and he had to tell me that Dan was a young man's name! I said, "Well, somebody ought to tell the girl so she can change her name!"

[Starts laughing again and won't stop. Whatever.]

[Meanwhile Sal and Carl have come in from the next room, and when they realize what Nan is laughing at, they start making fun of me again. Sal says this is just like how they would laugh together in the old days. Talk turns to pitching networks the idea of a reunion show. Nan tries her hand at an imitation of me with a girl's voice and points out that if they were doing this live, they would all have to keep a straight face somehow.]

[Switch off tape recorder.]

UPCOMING TITLES FROM GAVIN MENZIES, AUTHOR OF *1421: THE YEAR THE CHINESE DISCOVERED AMERICA*

Paul Tullis

1939: The Year Brazil Landed on the Moon

Relying on third-hand oral tradition, some drawings in dirt with a stick, and a rock that a Santeria priest says is a piece of the moon, or "space-stone," Menzies demonstrates that Armstrong, Aldrin, and the rest merely took a giant leap into the footsteps of a group of curious tourists from São Paulo. Lab tests as to the rock's origins were inconclusive, but Menzies says that just proves his case. "Since the lab couldn't identify it, the rock certainly must be from the moon," he writes.

1879: The Year Sicily Invented the Microchip

"Silicon," Menzies asserts, is a perverse Anglicization of "Sicily." "The stuff grows like a weed on the slopes of Mt. Etna," he reports. There's something for everyone in this volume, including the conspiracy theoriest: Gen. George S. Patton's belligerent insistence on conquering Messina before Britain's Montgomery could get there during World War II was just a shield for an American plan to keep knowledge of Sicily's achievement a secret from the rest of the world. "A little birdie told me," says Menzies.

1789: The French Revolution Wasn't Really French

Drawing chiefly on his own expertise as a connoisseur of *vin de pays* and his sister's recipe for risotto, which has a lovely tangy flavor he can't quite place but that goes nicely with the tarragon, Gavin Menzies contends that this whole business about the "French" Revolution "is totally a sham. It's so obviously Portuguese!" "Liberté, egalité, and fraternité aren't even French words," Menzies boldly declares. "The Académie Française refused to rebut my findings, which just goes to prove that they can't deny it." In an appendix for the American version of the book, apparently deemed too astonishing by its original English publishers, Menzies adds that the British Isles aren't really islands at all, but "tracts of land not as large as a continent, but surrounded by water."

250 B.C.: Hannibal Discovers Electricity

The early North Africans were grievously underestimated. Menzies says he has been to apartments in Tunis that are equipped with televisions and stereo equipment, that the number 250 times 7 ("more or less") equals 1752, the year Benjamin Franklin " 'claims' he 'discovered' 'electricity,' " and that 7 is Menzies's lucky number. Hannibal discovered electricity. Q.E.D.

621: That Was No Apple, It Was More Like a Dolma

Joining forces with David Hockney, who recently posited that Old Master painters used optical devices to achieve their stunningly accurate representation, Gavin Menzies asserts that it wasn't Newton at all who wrote *Principia,* but Mohammed. Yes, that Mohammed. When he wasn't busy taking dictation from God in a cave on the Arabian peninsula, the busy prophet was concocting the three laws of thermodynamics. Neither

Menzies nor Hockney can remember exactly what those are at the moment, but they will call when they do.

1844: The Year Native Americans Discovered Europe

Abandoning his prior assertions that China discovered America and that Europe soon followed, Menzies describes his recent discovery of patterns in ancient bison pelts which are "incontrovertible evidence" that neither Europeans nor Asians made it, in his words, "to the place we now know as 'North America'—which is really just a social construct, anyway, I mean, let's face it—until after a small band of Cherokee lesbians in canoes reached the shores of Ireland in 1844." Unfortunately they all immediately caught smallpox and died, which is why we have never heard their story until now. But a blacksmith named Perry knew the intrepid Cherokee women, managed not to catch smallpox from them, came to America, and never was heard from again. "Except," writes Menzies, "for the satellite transmission Perry made from his Lower East Side tenement to the Dakotas, where it was inscribed for eternity in the buffalo pelts." Menzies found the pelts at an antique store in Bergen County. "They were marked down," he recalls. "Or so I assumed."

GOOD WESTERNS, NOT PORN

Ross Barnes

Ace of the Saddle (1919)

Bad Man Bobbs (1915)

Between Men (1935)

Deadwood Dick (1940)

Garden of Eatin' (1943)

Gay Amigo, The (1949)

Gay Buckaroo, The (1932)

Hot Lead (1951)

Inside Straight (1951)

Man Rustlin' (1926)

Man to Man (1922)

Men in the Raw (1923)

One Shot Ross (1917)

Quigley Down Under (1990)

Ramrod (1947)

Rawhide Romance (1941)

Revenge of the Virgins (1966)

Rhythm of the Saddle (1938)

Ride a Wild Stud (1969)

Rimfire (1949)

There Was a Crooked Man ... (1970)

Valdez Is Coming (1971)

Wild West Whoopee (1931)

NORSE LEGENDS
REFERENCE PAGES

Kevin Guilfoile

EVERY DAY, it seems, one of your friends is forwarding another of those irritating Norse myths to your in-box. How can you tell which stories are true and which are traditional tales once used by the Nordic people to explain practices, beliefs, or natural phenomena? The Norse Legends Reference Pages are dedicated to separating *faktum* from *fiksjon,* and getting the straight dope from the mouths of people who know.

* * *

MYTH #1: In Valhalla, the Valkyries served mead, which poured in unending quantities from Odin's goat, Heidrun. They also served the warriors meat from the boar Saehrimnir, which the cook Andhrimnir would prepare by boiling it in the cauldron Eldhrimnir. The boar magically came back to life to be eaten again at the next meal.

FACT: "Oh wow, I'd forgotten about that," laughs former Valkyrie Hldissfrigg. "Some of the so-called warriors were actually getting squeamish about Andhrimnir slaughtering a pig every night—the squealing was really loud, I'll admit—so Odin came up with this tall one about an immortal 'magic boar,' and half those moron grunts totally bought it. I mean, the pigs didn't even look the same: one would have a big black spot, the next a little white one, or maybe he'd be pink instead of brown. It cracked us Valkyries up. I mean, if your boar was, in fact, magical—like maybe he could fly or pull a boat large enough to carry all the gods—would you really want to butcher, boil, and eat him over and over? Eventually you're gonna have a pissed-off magic hog all up in your face."

* * *

MYTH #2: The son of Odin and a member of the Aesir, Thor was the god of thunder and the main enemy of the giants. He would smash their heads with his mighty hammer Mjollnir. To wield this awesome weapon he needed iron gloves and a belt of strength. Mjollnir would return to Thor's hand after being thrown and was symbolic of lightning.

FACT: According to Heindall, who used to watch the Rainbow Bridge for the coming of the Frost Giants: "Well, his hammer was supposed to return to his hand after it was thrown, but that particular feature never really worked properly, and Thor wasted a lot of prime giant-killing time chasing the stupid thing up and down Middle Earth. I've heard some of the old-timers say Thor could have smashed the heads of about thirty or forty more giants, lifetime, if he only had a hammer with a decent return mechanism. I also asked him once about Mjollnir being symbolic of lightning and he rolled his eyes. 'I had a college girl tell me she did her thesis on how it was supposed to be some kind of penis,' he said. 'Sometimes a hammer is just a frigging hammer.' "

* * *

MYTH #3: Son of the giantess Rind, Valli was born for the sole purpose of avenging Baldur's death, since the gods could not kill one of their own. When he was only one day old, he killed Hodur. He will be one of the seven Aesir to survive the Ragnarok.

FACT: "One day old? Are you shitting me? Who told you that?" asks Tyr, ex–god of war and the inspiration for Tuesday. "God, that's hysterical. I mean, Hodur was blind, and maybe not the ripest grape on the vine, but he was Odin's kid. I'm pretty sure he could have fended off a newborn *baby*. Anyway, Valli'd been out of junior college for at least six years when he killed Hodur. He dropped out, but he blew off one summer on a Eurorail pass, and waited tables down in Cabo for a while. He had to have been at least 23 or 24. Geez. One day old? That's rich. When Loki hears that, he'll piss his pants."

*   *   *

MYTH #4: Hljod and Volsung had ten sons, the eldest named Sigmund, and one daughter named Signy. Volsung had a palace built around the tree called Branstock so that the massive trunk grew inside the palace walls. At Signy's wedding banquet, Odin arrived in his usual disguise—as an elderly man wearing a cape and hood. He stuck a sword in the tree and said that whichever man pulled out the sword could keep it. All tried but only Sigmund prevailed.

FACT: "In the first place, *everyone* knew it was Odin," says Njord, a guest at the banquet who, at the time, was god of the wind and sea. "He was always walking around in these disguises, but it was so obvious, even when he wore a wig and tried to cover up that gnarly empty socket. I mean, a crazy old man with one eye crashes your wedding and wants to show you a *sword trick*?—who else is it going to be? Anyway, Odin was all like 'Whosoever can pull this broadsword from the tree Branstock may possess it!' but he was so weak he could barely shove it in there and the crappy old thing fell out by itself at least a half-dozen times. The blade was all rusted out and no one wanted it, so Sigmund said to me, 'I'll pull the dumb sword out and make Odin happy if you catch the garter. I hate all this wedding crap.' "

*   *   *

MYTH #5: After Sigmund went into hiding, Signy exchanged shapes with a beautiful sorceress and went to her brother. The two slept together and Signy later had Sigmund's son, Sinfjotli.

FACT: According to Signy, "For the last time, I DID NOT SLEEP WITH MY BROTHER! Gross! But even if I wanted to, I wouldn't need to exchange shapes with any skank sorceress to do it. Sigmund was *always* trying to get me in bed. Lots of brothers and sisters were doing it back then because they thought the Ragnarok was coming, but I told him to go to Hel, so he keeps spreading this story that we knocked boots and he knows I won't defend myself and reveal the name of Sinfjotli's real father because the guy's married and weighing a run for county assessor. Sigmund is such a cock."

GOOFUS, GALLANT, RASHOMON

Jim Stallard

Ted, co-worker of Gallant:
That freak belonged to the cult of manners. Talk about a true believer. I rode on an airplane with him once, and he wouldn't start eating his meal until everyone was served.

Sheila, Goofus's high school classmate:
My memory of Goofus is that people saw what they wanted to. I was drawn to him because I sensed he was hurting inside. That's why he put up that wall and was "rude," but who's to say which way is right? It's just a social construct. Is there some cosmic, universal book of manners? I knew they'd find a way to make him pay, though. They always do.

Ronald, middle school classmate of both:
It was weird; they started at our school at the exact same time. Eighth grade. Everyone thought they were brothers, but it turns out their fathers were just transferred at the same time to the cereal plant in town. Gallant sits down in the front row

and starts sucking up to Mr. Anderson, the English teacher. Volunteers for everything, like our literary journal, *Chrysalis*—all that gay stuff.

Shawn, high school classmate of Goofus:
Goofus—my god, what a bad-boy poseur. I could tell he had picked up his Nietzscheism from a comic book. He would talk about the "Will to Power." But there was also some G. Gordon Liddy mixed in there. He loved doing the candle trick, moving his hand through the flame and pretending he didn't mind the pain. Then I did the same thing with my finger, showing him how full of shit he was.

Natalie, Gallant's high school friend:
Gallant was one of the few mature guys in our high school. Sensitive. We used to talk about James Taylor during lunch. I thought him the perfect gentleman, and of course my parents loved him. But when someone is polite to the point of having that Moonie quality, it gets to you. Finally it dawned on me that he used that politeness as a way of controlling me. That was what it was all about—he followed the rules because it gave him the advantage.

Alex, high school teacher of Goofus:
Goofus had a top-notch bullshit detector. Most teenagers think they have one, but his was the real thing, and I'm one of the few teachers who can relate to it. I introduced him to Kerouac, Bukowski, Burroughs. He acted enthusiastic about writing a paper in which they interacted. But it turned out to be seven pages of ... well, I was one of the characters in the scene, which was extremely graphic and not what we agreed on.

Paul, Gallant's college acquaintance:
Gallant just didn't get it when it came to relating to people. He would say words the "proper" way that no one normal ever does—you know, "Don't act immatoor." Always the authority.

One night I'm walking to dinner with him and another student, a friend from England, and we're ragging on each other—he's calling me Yank and I'm calling him Limey. Gallant breaks in to inform us that "Limey" comes from the British navy, eating limes to avoid scurvy, blah, blah, blah. Gee, thanks Gallant. Dork.

Brandon, junior college classmate of Goofus:
Was Goofus a rebel? He sure liked to think so. He cultivated that tousled hair thing. He wouldn't go out unless he thought it was prominent enough. I sat in his living room for forty-five minutes once waiting for him to sculpt it into the perfect unkempt shape. But that roughness was skin deep. I knew he'd be easy pickings in a real fight.

Dan, Gallant's college acquaintance:
Gallant would walk into a party and suck all the air out of the room. He would pretend not to be disapproving but he always made a point of commenting on what you were drinking, or how many you had—"You must really like that kind of beer"—until you edged away.

Darlene, ex-wife of Goofus:
I thought I could change Goofus. Remember, I'm a town girl who's never gone anywhere, and I was looking for some excitement. I had a lot to learn about men. With that electronic ankle bracelet, he couldn't leave the house after dark, so it was always me doing the shopping and running last-minute errands. And through all that he was always talking about how oppressed he was. Try raising three kids when your husband won't get off his ass.

Steve, Gallant's college acquaintance:
Gallant's attempts to seem cool were just painful. One time after making some incredibly lame joke he said, "I'm just breaking your balls," and the rest of us almost died laughing.

Shane, Goofus's army buddy:
Goofus loved Jack Daniel's. And Yukon Jack. He always wanted to do snakebites even though I don't think he liked them—just the name. He would do two and then switch to something else.

Brad, Gallant's co-worker:
Gallant was the total company man. There's not a buzzword he didn't use to death. We're at a strategy meeting one day and he actually says, "If you fail to plan, you plan to fail." I had to avoid making eye contact with Tony, another co-worker, because I knew we would both lose it and get in trouble.

Reverend John Swafford, Gallant's minister:
Gallant was a wonderful addition to our church. He always showed tremendous concern for the members, making inquiries and then letting me know which ones seemed to be having personal problems. If he had just had a little more concern for himself, things would not have turned out the way they did.

Harold, charity event organizer:
What happened was a disgrace. I put together nice events with the right kinds of people attending. I don't need this kind of publicity.

David, Gallant's co-worker:
I don't really understand what pushed Gallant over the edge. Serving from the right rather than the left—who even pays attention to that stuff? Especially at a fund-raiser. I think Gallant must have been on something. There's a side of him nobody knows. It's weird how everything came full circle, though. It was fate Goofus got assigned to serve that table.

Dean, fellow waiter with Goofus:
Goofus told me in the kitchen he had a bad feeling about that

night. It was weird because he's not usually superstitious. I was still in there putting garnishes on the plates when I heard the altercation—I just thought someone was getting chewed out for dropping a tray.

David, deputy mayor:
I was at the next table. Everything is normal. The waiters are bringing the entrées out and whisking the salads away. Suddenly, this nice-looking man at their table explodes in rage. He screams out "Right is wrong!" several times at this poor server who's looking at him in shock. Before anyone can move he puts one hand on top of the server's head, the other on his jaw, and just snaps his neck, Delta Force style. Then he sat back down and put his napkin in his lap.

Evan, Gallant's co-worker:
I was sitting across from Gallant. Goofus was baiting him—he was looking right at me with this smirk on his face while he set the plate down. Well, he got a reaction all right. I hope Goofus is happy wherever he is—where exactly do scum go when they die?

George, Gallant's co-worker:
Wow—a life sentence. Normally I'd say Gallant won't last a week on the inside. But I definitely can imagine him being very helpful to some inmate, if you get me.

Harold, cemetery custodian:
Goofus's tombstone is not marked well and is hard to find, but the teenage kids have started making pilgrimages to it. They go there and get drunk and weepy. I find their beer cans and wine bottles along with flowers and notes saying stuff like "You spoke the truth and they killed you for it." I'm thinking: You want to make him out to be your hero, go crazy, I don't care. Just don't leave your crap all over the ground for me to clean up. Didn't anybody ever teach these kids manners?

NOT-GOOD TITLES FOR
ROMANTIC FILMS

Tim Blair

Bob & Carol & Ted & Orrin

Fists of Fondness

Breakfast at Shoney's

Woman and Mandingo

Cat on a Hot Iron Grill

Lung Story

The Horse Renderer

Pretty Prostitute

Three Felonies and a Conviction

Elmo and I

It's Congenital!

Limbless in Seattle

Depriving Miss Daisy

Filthy Dancing

The Man Who Kissed Liberty Valance

Look Who's Shaking

Drugstore Cow

Romeo and Julio

BLACK, GRAY, GREEN, RED, BLUE: A LETTER FROM A FAMOUS PAINTER ON THE MOON

Ben Greenman

Dear Lucille Bogan,

Fifteen years ago, when I left the earth, I was just another struggling painter in New York City. My canvases were of two varieties: expressionistic black-and-gray cityscapes which often featured hunched figures collapsed inside oversized trench coats, and brightly colored nudes of you. One June day, I made up my mind to abandon the darker side of my nature and embrace what was good in the world. I came to your apartment and leaned on the buzzer. "Hello?" you said. "It's me," I said. We had dinner. We had dessert. We went to bed and drank a few glasses of red wine, after which I made my case for embracing what was good in the world. "You know what that means? For us?" I said. You seemed to. We went to sleep perpendicular to one another. Your head was on my chest. The next morning, when I woke up, I was on the moon. You were not. I cursed. I kicked a stone and it flew for what seemed like miles. Low gravity has its advantages. By noon, though, I had recovered my composure sufficiently to invent the style of painting that would bring me international—indeed, interplanetary—renown. It was brighter and more vivid, even, than the nudes. It exploded with color. Here on the moon that kind of thing was in great demand, and has continued to be.

*   *   *

Dear Lucille Bogan,

Four days ago here on the moon I fell and hit my head on the corner of a table. I got up almost immediately—low gravity has its advantages—but I had a dizzy spell, then a fainting spell, then a swoon. It turns out that the culprit was not the fall at all but rather a moderately severe case of something called Longtime Moon Resident Dissociative Disorder, or Lam-rod. Symptoms include slight dizziness. I'm going to go lie down for a moment.

*   *   *

Dear Lucille Bogan,

Another symptom of Lam-rod is that you tend to start letters over again even though you have started them already.

*   *   *

Dear Lucille Bogan,

Last night I went to see a friend of mine named Krystof Janikowski. He's here on the moon, too. Has been since ninety-two. He came here with his son Krystof Janikowski, Jr. Krystof Janikowski likes to call him "the Hebe dwarf" because I guess the mother is Jewish. Krystof Janikowski also likes to pretend that he hates his ex-wife although I happen to know that they had a perfectly amicable separation and that he still treasures her opinion on most matters. Krystof Janikowski wanted to discuss a book he has written. It's called *Blocaine and Shabu,* and it's a blaxploitation thriller set on the earth in which one guy does another guy a solid. Krystof Janikowski is a god-damned idiot, and I told him so, right in front of that Hebe dwarf. He took a swing at me, and landed a punch on my shoulder, but it barely hurt. Low gravity has its advantages.

*　*　*

Dear Lucille Bogan,

Another effect of Lam-rod is that you start to question yourself. This letter seems no more interesting to me than a Fabian milk report. And maybe *Blocaine and Shabu* isn't that bad after all.

*　*　*

Dear Lucille Bogan,

Or is it terrible? This Lam-rod is immensely frustrating. I am a famous artist. My work has been exhibited in the Art Museum of the Moon, the Modern Moon Art Museum, and the Lunar Art Institute. So why can't I render a confident and irrevocable judgment on the quality of *Blocaine and Shabu?* I am going to the doctor right now.

*　*　*

Dear Lucille Bogan,

The doctor, who was short and who would have been considered fat back when I was on earth but is now simply round—low gravity has its advantages—gave me a green pill. Doctors here on the moon are like that. They think that pills solve everything. When I was walking back from the doctor's office, I saw Krystof Janikowski. He turned to avoid me, but I went up to him and clapped him on the back. "You know," I said, "my opinion about the book is simply my opinion. If I had listened to every jerk who expressed skepticism during the three hours it took me to become a famous painter, I might have never done so." Krystof Janikowski laughed. "I know," he said. "But I appreciate your honesty. And I think I figured out the problem: I think the title should be reversed. *Shabu and Blocaine* is much better." I shrugged. It didn't seem to matter. So maybe the doctor and his green pill were the answer after all.

*   *   *

Dear Lucille Bogan,

Now it is tomorrow, and I am in such despair that I must call the doctor again.

*   *   *

Dear Lucille Bogan,

The doctor told me that despair is a side effect of the green pill. "First you feel real good," he said, "and then you feel real bad." I asked him why he didn't warn me about that before. "Because I am better friends with Krystof Janikowski," he said. "The Hebe dwarf is my godson." He laughed merrily. "You'll want to tear off your face all afternoon," he said, "but it should be gone by tomorrow."

*   *   *

Dear Lucille Bogan,

Now it is tomorrow again and I am in even greater despair. I called the doctor. "Crap," he said, and he rushed right over. He gave me a red pill and then began to take my pulse, to listen to my breathing, to palpate me about the neck and jaw. Then he stopped. "Whose paintings are these?" he said. I told him they were mine. "They are beautiful," he said. "Absolutely beautiful." I told him that I was famous. "I don't really follow the art world," he said. "But I know what I like. I especially like that one." I followed his finger and found that he was pointing toward a small canvas near the bookshelf. It was a foot square, hung at diamond angle. It was painted from memory. It was a portrait of you. At once, my despair lifted. Unfortunately, it was replaced by a crippling pain that radiated from my Adam's apple and quickly reached my head and my stomach. I fell to the ground, screaming. "Aha," the doctor said. "I think I know what the matter is." He produced a blue pill and threw it into the air. While it fell, he explained to me what he thought was happening; low gravity has its advantages. "The red pill," he said, "tends to dredge up emotional pain and then, when the source of that pain is identified, convert all psychological burden into acute physical pain." I asked him what the blue pill did. "Painkiller," he said, and left.

*　　*　　*

Dear Lucille Bogan,

Another effect of Lam-rod is that you tend to digress before you get to the point. Luckily, the red pill curbs that digressive effect somewhat. So this is the point: I miss you. I miss you terribly. I miss you horribly. I miss you painfully. I know that I am expressing myself clumsily. I am a painter, not a writer. I regret almost every second that has passed since I went to sleep on the earth and woke up on the moon. I was blithely unaware of how wretched and empty my life would feel without you. Remember? I cursed and kicked a stone. These are the behaviors of a child who has misplaced a toy, not a man who has been separated from a woman. Once, about a year ago, I was walking outside, and I saw Krystof Janikowski with Krystof Janikowski, Jr. This was when *Blocaine and Shabu* was just a glint in his eye; he talked about it, but he had not written a word. Krystof Janikowski was on his back on a blanket on the ground. He had his hands behind his head. He was sunbathing and listening to the radio. Krystof Janikowski, Jr., was running around, playing, making noise. Boys will be boys. But then that little Krystof Janikowski, Jr., came and lay down on the blanket. He tucked himself into the crook of his arm, and then he shifted so that he was perpendicular to his father. That little Hebe dwarf looked like he was in heaven. I started to cry. At the time, I had no idea why.

*   *   *

Dear Lucille Bogan,

This blue pill is making a fool of me. It does nothing. The pain is still in my throat and head and belly. I long for the days before the red pill, for the days when I was afflicted only with Lam-rod. And the despair has returned with even greater ferocity. Evidently the green pill works in cycles. This morning I dashed off a small painting, in dour black-and-gray, of a lone figure scuttling across a rainy alleyway. When I finished, I had a sudden urge to climb to the roof of my house and jump off. I didn't, though, because I would probably just float to the ground like a feather. Low gravity has its disadvantages.

LISTS

POSSIBLE FOLLOW-UP SONGS
FOR ONE-HIT WONDERS

John Moe

"How Are We Going to Get These Dogs Back In?"

"Bust an Additional Move"

"Seriously, Eileen, Come On"

"(Won't You Give Me a Ride Home from) Funkytown?"

"Remember When You Lit Up My Life? That Was Great"

"I Will Now Pass the Dutchie Back to You and Thank You for Passing It to Me Originally Because I Really Enjoyed the Dutchie"

"The Morning That the Lights Came Back On in Georgia"

"Everybody Was Kung Fu Making Up"

"Whoomp! There It Continues to Be"

"867–5309, Extension 2"

"We Never Took It and Persist in Our Refusal to Take It"

THIRTY GOOD NAMES FOR A DANCE TROUPE, INCLUDING FIVE THAT ARE ALREADY TAKEN BY ACTUAL TROUPES, AND TWO THAT ARE TAKEN BY CHEESES

Daniel Archer, Peter McGrath, and Jenny Traig

1. Dance on Tap

2. Classic Elegance*

3. Puttin' on the Glitz

4. Kinetic Rain

5. Classically Brilliant

6. The Daniel Archer Clog Explosion

7. Jazz in Our Pants

8. Off Our Meds

9. A Touch of Class*

10. Jazz Infection

11. Dance Blitzkrieg

12. I Stepped in Jazz

13. The Softshoe Experience

14. Jazzturbation

15. Dance Precisions*

16. Style in Motion

17. Prance Decisions

*Real dance troupe

197

18. Jazzy Garlic Jazz**

19. Clog Jam

20. The Hot Shot Two-Steppers

21. Planet Dance Rising Stars*

22. Beansteamin'

23. Jazz Packers

24. Young Organ Grinders

25. Help Me, I Think I'm … Dancing

26. Highland Odyssey

27. Jazz 'Em!

28. Step to the Real

29. Rondele**

30. Just Plain Dancin'*

*Real dance troupe
**Cheese

WAYS THIS ONE PROJECT MANAGER REPLIES TO MY REPLIES TO HER E-MAILED QUESTIONS ABOUT DOCUMENTATION

Peter Ward Brown

A million thanks, Peter.

Excellent and many thanks.

Thanks a million.

Sounds great … many thanks.

Many many thanks.

Thanks, Peter.

Thanks!

Many thanks.

Thanks much.

Ok. Thank you.

FIRST LINES TO BOOKS I WON'T WRITE

Jim Behrle

Michael Kindness slept.

In the end, as it was in the beginning and is now, I was a sad sack with time and a harmonica.

Being the last man on earth ain't all it's cracked up to be.

I keep asking myself, "Self, when am I going to get my wiffle ball back?"

"Would you like a bag with that?" the clerk asked clerkishly.

It was not the best of times— not by a long shot, Slappy.

Captain Picard and Commander Riker emerged from the Holodeck looking rather sour.

It is inevitable that the experience of knocking Noxzema facial cleansing cream to the bathroom floor reminds one of springtime, and hyacinths.

Nomar Garciaparra was born on July 23, 1973, in Whittier, California.

In retrospect, going back in time that time just to watch the Velvet Underground play at Max's Kansas City was a terrible, terrible idea.

"Ha ha ha ha ha ha ha ha ha ha ha ha ha ha ha ha ha ha ha ha ha ha ha ha ha ha ha ha ha," he thought.

On second thought, no.

Erin!

THINGS NYC CAB DRIVERS YELLED AT ME WHILE I CROSSED THE STREET

Jeff Hurlock

—Move it, you hump.

—You dumb man.

—Tell me this! Tell me this!

—Sunnuva-bam. Sons of bitches.

—I am trying to do this!

—Where are you going with this?

—Yankee, go home.

—You in my trouble yet, Mister?

—My lane.

—I'll take you to Queens.

LESSONS LEARNED FROM MY STUDY OF LITERATURE

Sean Carman

You think you know someone, then they go and do something you'd never expect.

Alcoholism has a sadly romantic quality that conventional attitudes overlook. Society = afraid to say this!

The thing about adultery is it's the highest expression of pure human freedom.

The true criminal mind = no remorse ever = not a bad way to live, really, when you think about it, especially compared to the way society lives.

No matter how hard you try, you can never get your mind around the concept of infinity. Same for time travel!

We hold deeply irreconcilable attitudes about our parents.

Children have the capacity to both frighten and delight.

Nothing is more precious than the love of a Scottish playwright, cowboy poet, or shy cartoonist.

No amount of tear-stained recriminations can change the fact that a loving mother-daughter relationship is the world's greatest gift.

As a rule, life's greatest opportunities come most often to down-and-out insurance salesman, highway drifters, and car mechanics.

ALL OF CHEWBACCA'S DIALOGUE IN THE COMIC BOOK VERSION OF *THE EMPIRE STRIKES BACK*

Brian McMullen

Raarghhh!   Rawrrk!

Waaark!   Nowrrrragh!

Vaaarrk!   Nrawwwwk!

Growwk!   Waaaaarrk!

Awwrk?   Yawrrrk!

Aowwww!   Raarghh!

Narowrrr?!   Varowrk!

Vowarrrk!

CAPITALIZED WORDS AND PHRASES APPEARING IN *THE OFFICIAL SEA-MONKEY HANDBOOK*

Amy L. Stender

AGAINST

ALIVE!

ANY TIME!

ANYTHING

ASTOUND

BACK TO LIFE

BACTERIA

BEHIND

BOY

BUT IT WORKS!

CANNOT LIVE

CAUTION

CAUTION

CHAIN OF LIFE

CHANCE

DO NOT FEED

DO NOT INTERFERE

DO NOT STIR!

DON'T

FAST

FRENZY

FRIEND!

FULLY MAN-MADE PETS

GIRL

HAPPEN

HATCH ALIVE

HUMAN BEINGS!

INSTANTLY

LIVE ACTORS AND ACTRESSES!

MAGICAL MOMENT

MALES

MANY TIMES LARGER THAN LIFE

MIRACLE

MORE

MORE

NEVER

NEW

NEW WORLD OF FUN

NOT

OBEY YOUR COMMANDS

ONE DAY

OTHER

OVERFEEDING

PEOPLE!

PET LOBSTER

REAL GAMES

RETURN TO LIFE

RISE!

SEA MEDIC

SEA-MONKEY BASEBALL

STAGGERS THE IMAGINATION!

STANDARD

STOP ALL FEEDING

SUPER

SUPER-ACTIVITY!

SUSPENDED ANIMATION!

THE CONTINUOUS PRODUCTION OF ADVANTAGEOUS COMBINATIONS OF "GENES"

TIME-TRAVELERS

TODAY!

TRICK

TWO HUNDRED FEET TALL

UPSTREAM

VERTEBRATES

WE HAVE FOUND THE SECRET OF TRAINING SEA-MONKEYS TO PLAY REAL GAMES WITH

BAD NAMES FOR BOATS

Jim Ruland

Shark Chum

Aquarium Furniture

Mullet King

Old Styrofoamsides

U.S.S. *Colander*

Torpedo Buddy

Narwussy

My Misunderstood Mussel

Sea Pinto

Crushed in the Tentacles of a Giant Squid

El Kaputo

Rime of the Ancient Tax Preparer

ACTUAL USER COMMENTS IN THE "FAT CATS" PHOTO GALLERY AT CUTECATS.COM

Blake Wirht

That's the fattest cat I've ever ever seen.

I have seen fatter.

That's not a fat cat!

How did he get this fat?????

It's either a moldy watermelon or a fluffy cow. I can't tell!

He's so cute! I bet he makes a snuggly cuddly squishy pillow!

Bob, did you rate these a 1?

Two paws up!

Seriously, I haven't any idea how hair got in your toothbrush!

Can I move to the bathtub now?

Hair didn't get in my toothbrush!! And that babe is very cute!

What is your deal? I did not throw the toilet paper down the drain!

AH! The light hurts!

Tu eres un elefante grande y un gato bonito! Pretty fat kitty!!!!!!

Sexy!

INEFFECTIVE WAYS TO SUBDUE A JAGUAR

Elizabeth Butler

Hit him with a sock full of pennies.

Bite him to make him think you're a jaguar.

Punch-punch-overhead kick combo.

Tell him that your mommy's not home.

Read from a biography of a former United States president in a soothing voice.

Quickly make a fake female jaguar and place it in front of a large, flat stone on which you've painted a doorway.

The four legs of a chair, all moving simultaneously.

Pat him on the back until he burps.

Death roll.

MUSIC INDUSTRY TRENDS NOT YET OVEREXPOSED

John Moe

Trance tuba

Self-deprecating hip-hop

All-dog bluegrass

Mild salsa

Teamsta rap

Immature adult contemporary

Back hair metal

Gangsta polka

Amino acid jazz

Despairaoke

Barbershop quartet–core

Psychedelic chamber groups

Hard on the outside but with a squishy nougat center–core

Graduate school rap

Halfway-house music

Reasonable speed metal

Jazz-crap fusion

Blank tapes

INTERNATIONAL EQUIVALENTS, CAKE HOLE

Aaron Stoker-Ring

Spain: flan hole

Germany: strudel hole

France: madeleine hole

Italy: cannoli hole

Austria: torte hole

Greece: baklava hole

Poland: babka hole

Russia: blini hole

Haiti: cane hole

India: ras malai hole

Malaysia: chendol hole

China: eight-treasure-pudding hole

England: trifle pit

ANIMALS I ENJOY IMAGINING
Felix Muhl

Human baby with wings and/or talons: these would be adorable and deadly.

No-toed sloth: like the three-toed sloth, but, you know.

Falcon with a shiny shell: a dark emerald green, and hard like armor. These would be so cool and also deadly.

Glowworms: I know these exist but I have never seen one. And can you believe it? Apparently they actually glow.

Tiny dinosaur, approximately thumb-size: like maybe a little brontosaurus in your palm?

Silkworms: do these really make silk or just some silklike mush? If they do in fact make silk, that's crazy.

Kittens with blue eyes and very soft paws: of course these are real and I have even seen and held and cuddled them. But still, they are great to think about.

EXPRESSIONS THAT VICTOR SKAARUP AND KRIS WINTHER THOUGHT FIT TO INCLUDE IN THEIR 1949 SWEDISH REFERENCE WORK *USA SLANG, ORDBOK OVER-MODERN AMERIKANSK SLANG*
Ethan Hein

all to the mustard

awry-eyed

baked wind

balcony owl

barbadacious

bun-yanker

catching the monk

dilly-mill

Dutch treat

geegawful

Mendelssohning

panther sweat

patch my pantywaist!

prunes, to be full of

putty blower

skibby

slither tuber

wavy navy

wooden nutmeg

X-legged

yard goose

RAPPER OR TOILETRY?
Mike Daulton[*]

1. Suave
2. Nice & Smooth
3. Soft & Gentle
4. Shyne
5. All Fresh
6. All Natural
7. Remedy
8. D-Flame
9. Cream Silk

10. Volume 10
11. Dimension
12. Cool Breeze
13. Smooth Appeal
14. Q-Tip

TOILETRY: 1, 3, 5, 9, 11, 13.
RAPPER: 2, 4, 6, 7, 8, 10, 12.
BOTH TOILETRY AND
RAPPER: 14.

[*]Tip of the hat to Chris Harris

WORDS USED BY MY GRANDFATHER IN HIS WWII DIARY TO DENOTE INTOXICATION
Elizabeth Ellen

gay

drunk

high

woozy

happy

soused

looped

plastered

ginned up

stinko

SIGNS ON THE LAWNS OF PEOPLE WHOSE LAWNS YOU MAY WANT TO AVOID

Rich Michaels and Jon Crawford

Beware of God.

Step to the left. A little more. A little more! Very good.

If you don't get off my lawn, I'll get off on you.

I LIKE SIGNS!!!

Keep off loose soil.

The Perot Family.

Mr. Vanilla Ice no longer lives here.

I squirt on your shoes from my special place.

I'm pleasuring you from the inside.

ACTUAL EXCERPTS FROM REUNION CHAT WEBSITE AUTOBIOGRAPHIES OF PITTSBURGH-AREA HIGH SCHOOL GRADUATES

Jessica Sedgewick

Unfortunately, I am still in Pittsburgh.

Find me at Yahoo. Please do not mention anything about Mormons!

I plan on doing some design work but my focus will always be on the fine arts I produce.

First off for all you wondering I am not a nun.

How my spouse and I met: My cousin had her friend pick me up from detention.

I GOT MARRIED IN 1999. I HAVE TO TAKE CARE OF ME.

I check my e-mail every few days. If you want more, it's up to you.

We are getting married in October 2002, much to his family's displeasure.

I was a drag queen for about two years, and I thought that I was gay. But I am not!

If you didn't like me, then I could care less if you're even reading this, let alone what you think.

I am now in New York City, living the turbulent and courageous life of a professional actor and playwright.

I'm always interested in seeing where/how everyone is doing, how many kids you now have, how many marriages you've been through, and how we each individually feed off one another's miserable existence in life.

I don't have wife. But I got my son. That all it matter. (I love to play golf and I'm pretty good.)

I have not yet married, but I am still with the father of my children.

Then after a rather embarrassing CB radio conversation, we had set up our first date.

I guess the most important thing is that I am happy and spanking more ass than ever.

FEATURED MENU ITEMS AT THE EXISTENTIALIST'S CAFÉ

Elizabeth Miller

Pasta cooked like hell

Pâté made from a duck that hates you

Gnocchi and nothingness

Salmon in sardonic sauce

Spanocrapita

Tarte de despair

Filet de tobacco

Crème de Camus

Le poulet is very bored tonight

Plate of butter

INTRODUCING THE NEW CEREALS

Amy O'Leary and Adam Weitz

Cracklin' Monkey Bran

Booty Loops

Graffiti Pebbles

Frosted Lying Bitch Squares

Abominations of the Raisin

Sweet Jesus Flakes

Oat Tolerance

Honey Bunches of Malaise

Nano Bran

Marshmallow Crispies of Ennui

Sugared Surgical Puffs

Morning-After Muesli

Hot Wheaty Meal

SCHOOLYARD GAMES FOR UNPOPULAR CHILDREN
Greg Knauss

Hide 'n' Be Lonely

Goose Goose Goose

Teeter

Unhappy-Go-Round

Kick the Can, Over and Over Again, Angrily

Studio Apartment

Very Easy Tag

NAMES OF SQUASH THAT ALSO MAKE GOOD TERMS OF ENDEARMENT
Laura Belous

Banana

Buttercup

Butternut

Delicata

Golden Nugget

Large Turban

Mini Turban

Pumpkin Pie

Puritan

Spaghetti

Sugar Loaf

Sweet Dumpling

THE LATEST IN INNUENDO BUMPER STICKERS
Jason Roberts

Feng Shui experts do it with strategically placed mirrors.

Outplacement consultants do it in what used to be your boss's office, right at the desk where he once called you an "invaluable asset" and hinted at a raise.

Medical marijuana–using glaucoma patients do it until they go blind, and even after, for the pain.

Working moms who think that keeping a journal will help them become mystery novelists get around to doing it only very occasionally.

Reunion attendees do it with a bittersweet sadness and sense of what might have been, if only they had known how beautiful they truly were when young.

Ex-teachers regret doing it with class.

LAST NAMES THAT ARE MORE COMMON THAN MY OWN, ACCORDING TO THE CENSUS BUREAU

Seth Kolloen

Crisafulli

Zwickl

Penix

Luttenegger

Froschheiser

Dabdoub

Gothro

Mutschelknaus

Schrumph

Schroot

Schremp

Kraskouskas

Bitler

MNEMONIC DEVICES TO HELP YOU REMEMBER HOW TO SPELL "MNEMONIC DEVICES"

Rick Larsen

My Nephew Eats Many Oranges, Never Indicating Conscious Dismay—Even Vigorously Ingesting Certain Excessive Sizes.

Many Nations Embrace Making Overt Name-calling Illegal; Conversely, Dale Evans Viewed Internal Conflicts as External Symptoms.

Mike Nesmith Ended Monkees Over Nebulous Internal Complications. Davy, Evidently Victorious, Insisted Company Equally Share.

Much Noise Emitted Means Often Nothing. If Cabled Device Exceeds Voltage Indicated, Connect Extra Speakers.

Multi-National Energy Meetings Overlook Numerous Industrial Causes. Delays, Even Very Infinitesimal, Can Entangle Statesman.

NAMES CONSIDERED AND REJECTED BY THE SOFTWARE COMPANY "CISIVE" WHILE LOOKING FOR SOMETHING IN THE STYLE OF "TELIGENT" AND "GENUITY"

Earl L. Humphreys

Ane	Quisition
Cestuous	Sipid
Donesian	Stitutionalize
Dustrial	Terrobang
Fantile	Toxicant
Fectious	Troversion
Kblot	Tumesce
Nards	

THE LATEST IN FAKE MEAT PRODUCTS

Danielle Hess and Mickey Hess

Falseage Links	Venisoy
Looney Tuna	That Which Is Not Lamb
Soylisbury Fake	Beef Fauxganoff
Replicarcass	Pork Pretender
Replicacciatore	Chimpostor!
Not-Real Veal	Nostrich Burger
Fibber Liver	

ACTUALLY HEARD ON THE NEW YORK SUBWAY/NEVER HEARD ON THE NEW YORK SUBWAY

John Parsley

ACTUALLY HEARD:

"You all got legs, help a brother with one leg out."

"Come on man, that's my head you're hitting."

"Merry fucking Christmas."

"Two Dura-gizers, one dollar."

"Ladies and gentlemen, I am a blind accordion player. I am here to entertain you on the train."

"Jesus Christ is the redeemer, let him redeem you with his Christliness, Jesus he will. Yes."

"Excuse me, can I sit there? I'm going to ralph."

"I love SubTalk, 'cause I get to see all those poet guys and stuff."

"I'm on Fifth Avenue. That noise in the background? No, that's just some guy with a loudspeaker."

NEVER HEARD:

"When I sneeze I will aim my nose at my own jacket so as to spare you a sticky mess."

"No, that was definitely me. I will remove myself from your presence at the very next stop."

"I'm sorry that I'm brushing up against you; I do not want you, and if I could put my ass anywhere else, trust me, I would."

"Ladies and gentlemen, hold on tight; there's a train ahead and we're bustin' on through."

"Don't worry, I'll be cleaning this up as soon as I'm done."

"Mommy, can I be quiet now?"

LESS POPULAR BOARD GAMES

Neil Chamberlain

Slumlord

Mathemagic

Ennui

Chute and Chute

Fourth Reich

Kashlonk!

Scott Baio's Haunted House

Cannibal Adventure

Really Fucking Sorry

Tax Cheat

Electronic Swearing Battleship

Prostate Operation

Negro League Championship

Spork Factory

Rock 'Em Sock 'Em Spouses

Gajoink!

For the Love of God, Don't Wake Daddy!

Pet Rock Divorce Court

Desperation

Abrasive Egg-Timer Challenge

Save the Guggenheim!

Uncle Wiggily Is Dead

Monopoly with Grape Juice All Over It and the Goddamn Chance Cards All Stuck Together

REGRETTABLE PUNS I'VE USED AS HEADLINES AT THE IN-FLIGHT MAGAZINE FOR WHICH I WORK

Ross McCammon

Snow Time Like the Present

Inn-Capsulated

High Tee

And Don't Call Them Shorely

Hooks, Lines, and Thinkers

Noir Town

Hour of Braise

What's Kneaded

Oui Like

Too Much of a Food Thing

Raising the Steaks

Tea Wrecks

Polar Wheres

A Cramp and Your Stylus

CAUSE-AND-EFFECT RULES FOR SIDEWALK TRAVEL

John Moe

Step on a crack, break your mother's back.

Step on a line, break your father's spine.

Step on a flea, become a sucker MC.

Step on some dirt, move in with William Hurt.

Step on a rock, lose your favorite frock.

Step on a bee, become a sucker MC.

Step on a plant, remember Adam Ant?

Step on some grass, hey, get off the grass!

Step on a lime, travel back in time.

Step on a crack vial, break your mother's back vial.

Step on a twig, listen to Edvard Grieg.

Step on a tree, become a sucker MC.

Step on a curb, use a passive verb.

Step on Joyce DeWitt, throw a hysterical fit.

Step on some paper, solve a thrilling caper.

Step on some cardboard, change your name to "Mardboard."

Step on some trash, get way into Graham Nash.

Step on a sucker MC, hey, wow, good job!

CORPORATE MASCOTS: THEIR STUNNING SECRETS REVEALED

Daniel A. Brennan

Mr. Salty: Uses foul language

Cap'n Crunch: Severely disciplined for role in Tailhook scandal

Mr. Peanut: Often appears in public without pants

Ronald McDonald: Embarrassing association with serial killer/clown portraitist John Wayne Gacy

Snuggles, the Fabric Softener Bear: Shot a man in Reno just to watch him die

Rich Uncle Moneybags: Wanted in Atlantic City in connection with bank fraud, pageant-fixing

The Pep Boys (Manny, Moe, and Jack): Actually quite lethargic

Mr. Coffee: Beneficiary of a mob-established bank account at Bowery Savings Bank; used to beat up Mrs. Coffee

Jolly Green Giant: Easily misunderstood catchphrase has

been the cause of several arrests for solicitation

Charlie the Tuna: Frequently wakes up in tears at three in the morning, an empty bottle of bourbon on the nightstand, cigarette butts on the floor, another girl he doesn't recognize lying beside him. He tiptoes to the bathroom, stuffing a towel under the door to block out the sound and weeps into the sink, whispering the words "Oh God, please help me" over and over until the crying stops.

Mr. Softee: Impotent

ELEVEN LUNCH MEATS I HAVE INVENTED

Steven Tomsik

Brumschlagen	Hammed Beef
Cran-pepper Hen Loaf	Meatwurst
Spiced Saucetail	Head Tongue
Nippleroni	Buffalami
Fleen	There Are Five
Taste It	

SLOGANS OF NOT-SO-PRESTIGIOUS SCHOOLS

Jeff Johnson

Radclift: We're only a couple of letters away from being a really good school.

Mortensen Taxidermy: Let's not kid each other. You weren't our first choice, either.

Mike's Dental School: No lawsuits in nineteen months.

Williamsburg Institute: You can either live on campus or do it by mail.

Raymond Wright College: A lot of sodomy happens here. Yep, sodomy and free gum.

Duncan College: At Duncan College, your parents never see your report card. Guaranteed.

Chounter's Culinary College: You're not a student at Chounter, you're a junior teacher.

Rinzen Music* Academy:

---

*and forestry

People's Choice Junior College: At PCJC, we aren't afraid to have *TV Guide* in our media center.

Furrer Bible College: Did you know some translations of the Bible endorse weed smoking? How about free video rentals?

Colombia University: Porque parece un error tipográfico en su curriculum vitae.

SUBJECTS MY DAD DOESN'T LIKE AND WILL DISCUSS AT LENGTH IF RAISED

Kate Harris

Peacocks

The blue rug my mother bought for the front room

People borrowing things from his shed

The motion picture *Who Framed Roger Rabbit*

Food courts

Sugar that has been spilled on the kitchen tiles

Alternative medicine

The fact that the cat is putting on weight

Odors that can't be explained

INFREQUENTLY ASKED QUESTIONS

Justin Dobbs

Can I top off your warm salt water?

Does this sound infected?

Who's her favorite bass player?

Why is your spleen like that?

Is he going to perpetuate that misconception all night?

But how do you get it to float next to the VCR?

Why brown?

Did you say "Massachusetts"?

Was that when you noticed my uncle's birthmark?

When does the next Frenchman go by here?

Who said anything about yachting?

Isn't that the guy from the Psychedelic Furs?

Why was that written?

What's with the hedge trimmer?

Could you please stop looking at my bowling trophy?

You call yourself a witch doctor?

Couldn't you at least have buried the can opener?

What do you know from black lung?

More duck sauce?

Who dat talkin' 'bout beatin' dem Bengals?

RECENTLY DISCOVERED VOTING IRREGULARITIES IN FLORIDA

John Moe

Voters driven to polls by friend Jason, despite hating Jason

Self-loathing in Broward County

98 percent of votes in Santarosa County cast for Stalin

Unapproved "Gore eats old people" yard signs

All Gore voters statewide accidentally falling in front of trucks

Evidence of chicanery by infamous Miami Sound Machine

Democrats forced to vote in special "chamber of mice" booth

All 3,756 Gore daughters dressing as elderly women and voting in West Palm Beach

Casting an all-Democrat ballot forms the face of Satan on punch card

"Weird" feeling in Walton and Okaloosa Counties

"Weird" Al Yankovic in Hendry County

Ralph Nader

Everything being stupid and sucking

FILMS ABOUT TOUGH JEWS
Adam Weitz

The Ten Commandments
Casino

ACTUAL RESPONSES BY MY FOURTEEN-YEAR-OLD JAPANESE STUDENTS TO THE PROMPT "IN THE FUTURE, I WANT TO BE ..." AND "BECAUSE ..."
Brook Crowley

In the future, I want to be ... a makeup teacher
because ... I like makeup.

In the future, I want to be ... a worker
because ... the worker looks great.

In the future, I want to be ... eat egg
because ... eat egg.

In the future, I want to be ... a dog
because ...

In the future, I want to be ... a father
because ... I am a boy.

In the future, I want to be ... bogs
because ... bogs is interesting and very furry.

In the future, I want to be ... a public servant
because ... looks interesting.

In the future, I want to be ... a candy store
because ... I like cake.

In the future, I want to be ... child welfare
because ... I like childs.

In the future, I want to be ... a nurse
because ... help for men.

In the future, I want to be ... hairdresser
because ... it's cool.

In the future, I want to be … a dog
because … it's interesting.

In the future, I want to be … a clerk
because … I think it fits me.

In the future, I want to be … a postman
because … I can send dreams.

A LIST OF HIT TRACKS BY MY ELEVEN-YEAR-OLD SISTER, RUTH, WHOSE KNOWLEDGE OF METAL AND GLAM ROCK STEMS ENTIRELY FROM THE COVER OF A "NELSON AND NELSON SMOKIN' GUITAR LICKS" VIDEO WE SAW AT THE MUSIC STORE, BUT WHO, NEVERTHELESS, CALLING HERSELF "THE BLAST OFF!," DECIDED TO FORM HER OWN ENSEMBLE, "LUMPEE & MEEN," WHICH SHE WAS KIND ENOUGH TO LET ME JOIN

Leif and Ruth Larsen

"AAHHHHHHHHHHHHHHHHHHH, Great!!!"

"I'm Going to Antler You!!!"

"I'm Going to Antler You! (acoustic love-ballad remix)"

"I Should Have Washed My Hands…."

"The 'Teaparty of Darkness Which Is in My Head' Song"

"Mumsy!"

"Broken $237.99 Guitar!!!"

"Ruth, Wipe Your Chin, You're Dripping—You Look Like a Person Who's Not, You Know, Mentally Stable …!!!!"*

*props to our mom

TERRIBLE NAMES FOR HAIR SALONS

John Moe

Shear Hostility

Mane-lining Hair-oin

Clipping Penalty

Dexa-Trims

I Will Cut Your Head

Gut the Hell Out of Hair

The Razor's Edge Starring Bill Murray

The Mane Reason My Parole Was Revoked

Nervous McStabby's Hair Care Place

Reason Has Been E-Clips-ed by Rage

Running with Scissors

Armon Gilliam's House of Style

In No Conditioner to Drive

Hari Commandant

Cuts & Bruises

Dude, I'm So Buzzed

The Viet-Mane War Memorial

Get the Hell Out of Hair, Kevin

I Hate My Mother

George Hair-ison's Solo Career

Why Won't You Dye?

Los Angeles Clippers

Mein Coif

GOOD NAMES FOR HAMSTERS

Diana Fischer

Mrs. Leonard Pannaggio

Hammy

Chief

Mario

Drew Bledsoe

Toes

BAD NAMES FOR HAMSTERS

Diana Fischer

Seth

Gary

Judy

Joyce

Janice

Sandy Jacobson

The Dude

BABY NAMES FOR AN EXPECTED SISTER SUGGESTED BY NATHANIEL WATSON, AGE SIX

Sarah Brown

Pancake*	Jimmy II
Hambone*	Anna
Skeleton*	Hanna
Toto	Total Annihilation

*Name also suggested earlier for Watson's brother Jimmy, twenty-one-months old

BAD NAMES FOR PROFESSIONAL WRESTLERS— THE NEXT GENERATION

Jeff Johnson

Beckett	Butterscotch
The Tadpole	The Standoffish Person
Roy Cohn, Jr.	The Wooden Marmoset
The Splendid Splinter	The Pasty Accountant
Bruce the Spruce	The Tardy Worker
The Cuddler	Alan Dershowitz
The Framingham Fry Cook	Inky
Paula	The Soothsayer
Hamilton Jordan	The City Manager
Tarkanian	The Bench Warmer
The Sea Horse	The Plum-Eating Bastard
The Incontinent Minstrel	The Corpse
The Drooling Lamb	The Marionette

The Martyr

The Peppermint Rube

The Gout-Stepper

The Willamette Pimp

MORE BAD NAMES FOR
PROFESSIONAL WRESTLERS
(added 1:34 p.m. Wednesday)
Jeff Johnson

The Vegan

The Lonely Marine

Grace Kelly

Peter Billingsley

Swimmer's Itch

The Orderly

Smarty Pants

Babette

Jivamukti

Paul McCartney

The Shlub

The Shrill Housewife

The Truant Officer

The Dartmouth Grad Student

The Keokuk Optometrist

The Whispering Mime

Aaron Copland

The Impressionist

The Phonics Expert

Nancy Walker

Hospice Boy

Noel Coward

Frondeur

The Demimonde

The Victim

The Tattletale

Truffle

Victor Kiam

The Poet Laureate

Mrs. Grundy

Burt Hooton

The Pawn

Dale

The Little Ragu

Morrissey

AILMENTS I WILL PROBABLY HAVE, LATER

Steven Tomsik

Esophageal constricticitis

Temporal saturation of Creen's gland

Torso failure

Phlandibicules, as a result of Blaser's syndrome

Ocular swelling and general carbuncular pupil reflex

Degenerative anterior glandulae meialis humera, subsequent wens

Toxic spermatoceliosis

Goslee tooth

Ventricular hiatus, chestaxia, epidermal foam

Carditis in quadrant IV with nonmedianus hyphloxiatricine tark

Cementy ear

POSSIBLE CLOSING LINES FOR A DEFENDANT WHO HAS CHOSEN TO REPRESENT HIMSELF

Brian Sack

"My client professes his innocence. And when I look in the mirror and see his eyes, I just have to believe him."

"The facts, which I will present to you, will show that the defendant is not guilty. My client was nowhere near the scene of the crime. My client was where I was, obviously, because he is me, and I'm definitely aware of our whereabouts that night."

"Truth be told, no one knows what really happened that night. Except me and my client."

"I have been accused of a terrible crime. This frightens me both as a defendant and as a lawyer. I don't want to go to jail, and I'd hate to lose my first case."

"When all is said and done, you will have to take all the evidence and go into the room back there, talk about it, and decide amongst yourselves on a verdict and whatnot. Right?"

"I want you to take a good hard look at my client. I want you to ask yourself if he could be capable of such a heinous crime. But I don't want you to take that long hard look just yet, because it will distract me and I'm not finished talking."

SEVERAL PHRASES THAT HAVE NEVER BEEN UTTERED IN HUMAN HISTORY
Marshall Sella

"Look out, God—behind You!"

"Nothing's the same since Julie started those wars."

"The New World has that New World smell."

"We, the jury, find the defendant cute as a button."

"Shoot him again, Mr. President. He doesn't mind."

"Yummy plague!"

"I claim this land in the name of Phyllis T. Brunell."

"Let the ant-shaving begin!"

"No man is so tall as when he stoops to help a child kill."

"That was no lady, that was Iraq."

THINGS PEOPLE SAID TO ME WHILE I WORKED THE FRONT DESK OF AN OFFICE IN LIEU OF "WOULD YOU THROW THIS AWAY FOR ME?"
Sarah Brown

"I've got a present for you!"

"Think fast!"

"Here."

"Got a little something for you."

"Just because I like you so much …"

"Do you have trash under there?"

"Thanks."

"Aw, I got this just for you, Sarah!"

"Would you mind?"

"Watch out, this might be sticky."

REJECTED ARCADE GAMES
Jules Lipoff

Temporarily Disabling
Kombat

Falafel Time

Extreme Lawnmowing

The Congressional Redistrictor

Washing Machine 2: Another
Load before Bed

Street Panhandler Turbo

The 401(k) Adventure

Martha Stewart's Weed-Out!!

Rabbi Rendezvous: The
Circumcisions

Mule Kong, Jr.

Cheatin' Wife Hunter

THREE LITTLE THINGS I REGRET HAVING SAID
Dan Kennedy

"How's it doin'?"

—To Karen McGrew at
Nieblas Intermediate School,
Fountain Valley, CA, 1979

"Let's call up it some night!"

—To prospective employer
upon discovering we shared an
interest in Museum of

Television and Radio screening
of Superbowl commercials

"You think that's dick?"

—To street vendor upon
confronting him regarding a
joke he made about me as I
walked past

FOUR THINGS I WOULD HAVE SAID TO SYLVIA PLATH IF I HAD BEEN HER BOYFRIEND
Dan Kennedy

"Does something always have
to be wrong?"

"I'm so sick of you twisting my
words around."

"Nothing makes you happy."

"Maybe we should just break
up then."

THE EMPEROR HAS NO CORTEX: 100 PERCENT TRUE QUOTES FROM MY FORMER HOLLYWOOD BOSSES

Tom O'Connor

"It is my theory that it's people that make movies. They don't make themselves."

"I'm not asking you to reinvent the wheel, I'm asking you to reinvent a wheel."

"Are you sure this is a Christmas movie, just because the story happens during Christmas?"

"We need to create a matrix that sets up a pattern."

"There is something either not important or psychologically interesting about what you just said."

"I don't want to understand it, I just want to know how it's going to be done."

"You're too enthusiastic and eager to please. Every time I see you smile, it ruins my whole day."

"We're all familiar with the Linear Enmeshment Method of working toward production."

"I hear a clock ticking that I've never heard before … in my head."

"The thing that makes this script unique is that the characters travel back in time."

"Dreamworks doesn't have the imagination to talk to us."

"Development is not a business. Talking is not a business. Cash flow is a business."

"When I came in, this company was like a beheaded chicken. It was running around, had lots of energy, but no direction, no focus."

"He's a new director. Yes, he is French … but he's not French French."

"Let's make sure we're not dancing to their bagpiper."

"I need an office in New York too because there is a different ambiance there. It is more direct and less bigger-than-life than L.A. More rifle, less shotgun."

"Is there any way we can work Meat Loaf into this movie? He really represents the true spirit of it."

"Small words are so important in contracts."

TERMS USED IN AN OFFICE-SUPPLY CATALOG TO DESCRIBE PLACEMENTS OF TABS ON MANILA FILE FOLDERS THAT COULD ALSO BE USED TO DESCRIBE POLITICAL IDEOLOGIES OR SEXUAL PREFERENCES

Stephanie McNutt

Straight	Extreme Right
1st Position	Right of Center
2nd Position	2/5 Straight
3rd Position	

ALTERNATE TITLES
PROPOSED FOR THIS BOOK

Whimsical Is the New Weightiness
Humor Is Timeless: 1998–2003
The French Lieutenant's Woman
667: The Neighbor of the Beast
The Sound and So Forth
We're in the Library of Congress! We're in the Library of Congress!
A Child's Garden of Funnies
How Can It Be Irony When It Is Exactly What You Expected?
A Child's Garden of McSweeney's Erotica
The Only Book Ever Published
Necronomicon
Ow, Motherfucker!

CONTRIBUTORS

Jeff Alexander wishes Tom Bissell luck beating that indecent-exposure rap. He lives in Bukhara.

As a young boy, **Daniel "Fosse!" Archer** perfected the art of Jazz Hands. Over the years he has added the Jazz Drag, Fan Kick, and Ball Change to his repertoire. So far, no one seems impressed. He credits Debbie Allen, Lee Remick, and the 1983 blockbuster film *Stayin' Alive* for helping him develop a passion for the dance.

Stephany Aulenback lives in Nova Scotia.

Chris Bachelder received an M.F.A. from the University of Florida and now teaches writing and literature at Colorado College in Colorado Springs. He is the author of *Bear v. Shark: The Novel.*

Ross Alan Barnes attends Knox College in Galesburg, Illinois.

Jim Behrle edits can we have our ball back? on the web and is the Events Director at WordsWorth Books in Cambridge, Massachusetts.

Tom Bissell is the author of *Chasing the Sea* and lives in New York City. Since the day Mr. Alexander correctly identified Glorfindel as the elf whom Strider and the Hobbits meet on the way to Rivendell, he has deferred to his co-author on all things Tolkien.

Michael Ian Black lives in New York City.

Tim Blair is a columnist for *The Bulletin* magazine in Sydney, Australia, where he is free to roam, free of the dictates of French law, because he does live in France.

Zev Borow writes for magazines and for television and for love.

Arthur Bradford wrote a book called *Dogwalker* (Knopf, 2001) and directed a movie called *How's Your News?* (HBO, 2002). He lives with his grandmother.

Daniel A. Brennan resides in New York, where he trains Rhode Island Red bantams for competitive fighting exhibitions.

Brodie H. Brockie is the co-creator of capnwacky.com and makes movies and sketch comedy with A Monkey & A Type-writer Productions.

Peter Ward Brown lives in Columbus, Ohio, where he works in a gray cubicle that is almost in the corner.

Sarah Brown is a writer from Tulsa, Oklahoma, and has the strength of a bear that has the strength of two bears. She would love to meet your brother.

Sean Carman is an environmental lawyer in Seattle and, less frequently, a freelance writer and photographer.

Tim Carvell lives in New York, and has written for the *New York Times, Business 2.0, Fortune, Esquire,* and *Sports Illustrated for Women,* for whom he edited their swimtrunk issue. This is not a lie.

Sean Condon was born in Australia in 1965 and moved to Amsterdam in 1998, then reluctantly, moved back to Australia in 2003. He is the author of four novels, none of which is very popular. He is currently working on a fifth.

Mike Daulton works as an environmental lobbyist in Washington, D.C. This is his first published work. He has a wonderful girlfriend named Christina.

Justin Dobbs worked as a bartender for nine years before finding sport in the highly respected field of ad writing. Since then, his work has appeared in *Rolling Stone, Playboy,* and the classified section of *Peanut Farmer.* He lives in midtown Memphis with the wife.

More of **Elizabeth Ellen**'s writing can be found in *Monkeybicycle, Eyeshot, Pindeldyboz,* and *Surgery of Modern Warfare.* At the moment she resides in Michigan.

Peter Ferland is a screenwriter living in Los Angeles with his wife and two sons. He has only served jury duty once and wasn't selected for a trial.

T. G. Gibbon was born in Philadelphia and hopes to die there a century from now.

Ben Greenman is an editor at *The New Yorker* and the author of *Superbad* and *Superworse.* His fiction and humor pieces have appeared in *The Paris Review, The Mississippi Review, Mother Jones,* and elsewhere. He lives in Brooklyn.

Kevin Guilfoile is the co-author (with John Warner) of *My First Presidentiary: A Scrapbook by George W. Bush.* His work has appeared in *The New Republic, Business 2.0, Yahoo! Internet Life,* and *Maxim,* and he is a regular contributor to themorning news.org.

Ethan Hein is a musician living in New York City. He can currently be heard playing guitar, mandolin, harmonica, and other instruments in various bands.

Danielle Hess draws and paints, and works in a computer lab. This is the only thing she has written.

Mickey Hess is the author of the books *Big Wheel at the Cracker Factory, El Cumpleaños de Paco,* and *Nobody Likes a Smartass.* Read more about them at www.mickeyhess.net.

John Hodgman is a Former Professional Literary Agent and host of the Little Gray Book Lectures of Brooklyn. He is available to speak to your group, corporate retreat, family reunion, or other gathering on the subjects of publishing, writing, monster hunting, crime solving, the life cycle of oysters, the history of medicinal bitters and potions, *The Lord of the Rings,* and any other subject.

Earl L. Humphreys lives in Houston, Texas. This is his first published work.

Jeff Hurlock is a native of Hockessin, Delaware. Delaware is the First State.

Jeff Johnson has fought crime—with a smile—on the Eastern Seaboard since 1979.

Brian Kennedy lives in Washington, D.C., where he attends graduate school and works part-time at the Center for Strategic and International Studies.

Dan Kennedy is the author of *Loser Goes First* and an editor at ReallySmallTalk.com. He lives and works in New York City.

Greg Knauss has written for Suck.com, *Worth* magazine, and Playboy.com, among others. He lives in Los Angeles.

As a humor writer, **Rick Larsen** uses math every day. In 1973, he began spelling his last name with an "e."

Jules Lipoff recently graduated from Yale with a degree in molecular biophysics and biochemistry. His last two years, he was chairman of the *Yale Record,* the nation's oldest college humor magazine.

Kurt Luchs (kurtluchs@aol.com) manages a radio comedy syndicator called the American Comedy Network (www. americancomedynetwork.com). He also contributes to *The Onion, The New Yorker, McSweeney's,* and *The Late Late Show,* edits *The Big Jewel* (www.thebigjewel.com), and writes screenplays and books. His hobbies include volunteering at soup kitchens, rescuing injured condors, climbing Mount Everest, and being a pathological liar.

Ross McCammon lives in Chicago, where he works as a freelance writer and as an editor for an in-flight magazine in which he still includes the occasional regrettable pun.

Peter McGrath is an office worker in Washington, D.C. His hobbies include finding fault and eating food that he has prepared for himself.

Brian McMullen collects paperback copies of Wayne W. Dyer's *Your Erroneous Zones.* If you have a copy (or a lead on how to get a copy), please e-mail brianmcmullen@hotmail.com.

Stephanie McNutt, 21, is surprisingly convinced of her own worldliness despite having never resided outside a tri-county area in southeastern Wisconsin. She hopes you are happy now.

Elizabeth Miller lives in Portland, Oregon. She is married to a man named David, with whom she used to play in a Patsy Cline cover band. Her favorite skate trick combination is the blunt-slide to 5–0 shove-it.

John Moe is a writer, playwright, and radio producer in Seattle, Washington. His writing has appeared on Amazon.com, National Public Radio, and a few other media outlets. He clumsily operates the blog Monkey Disaster (monkeydisaster. blogspot.com). He is a father of two and a husband of one.

Christopher Monks lives in Massachusetts with his wife and two sons. His stories have appeared in several online literary journals, including *Eyeshot, Haypenny,* and *Pindeldyboz.* For more info please visit his website www.utterwonder.com.

Felix Muhl lives alone in the country.

Tom O'Connor is a writer, comedian, and fan of a baseball team. He lives in Los Angeles.

Mark O'Donnell's novels include *Getting Over Homer* and *Let Nothing You Dismay,* both of which make lovely gifts. He recently won a Tony award for writing the book of *Hairspray,* the Broadway musical.

Amy M. O'Leary is the co-author of *WAP Development with WML and WMLScript,* published by Macmillan. She is a radio documentarian.

Alysia Gray Painter lives in Los Angeles. Her work has appeared in *Bark* magazine, ModernHumorist.com, *101 Damnations, Dog is My Co-Pilot,* and volumes two and three of *Mirth of a Nation.*

John Parsley's writing has appeared in *Salon,* on *Northeast Public Radio,* and on countless, yet-to-be-combined scraps of paper product. He is an editor living in New York.

Keith Pille really, really liked Led Zeppelin in high school. After leaving for college, he decided that they sucked. As he approaches thirty, he suddenly finds himself liking them again. Living in south Minneapolis with his wife and two cats (none of whom have any use at all for the Zep), he is distressed to see the same thing happening with Pink Floyd.

Neal Pollack is the author of three books: the rock novel *Never Mind the Pollacks, Beneath the Axis Of Evil,* and *The Neal Pollack Anthology of American Literature,* which was originally published by McSweeney's Books and won the 2001 Firecracker Award for fiction. He writes for many publications, including *Vanity Fair,* the *New York Times,* and *Slate,* and updates his website, www.nealpollack.com, daily with political and literary satire. His band, the Neal Pollack Invasion, recently released its first album on The Telegraph Company Records. He lives in Austin, Texas.

Greg Purcell's poetry has appeared in *Fence, The Exquisite Corpse,* and *New American Writing.* With Joel Craig, he coordinates the Danny's Reading Series in Chicago. He believes that the further one's chemistry is off, the more painfully one believes in love. He is on at about half-beaker right now.

Todd Pruzan is an editor at *Print.* His book *The Clumsiest People in Europe,* a collaboration with a dead children's writer, is forthcoming from Bloomsbury USA.

Andy Rathbun goes to sleep around 11 p.m.

Jason Roberts writes in a former Dog and Cat Hospital in downtown San Francisco. His nonfiction book, tentatively entitled *The Gentleman in the Distance,* is forthcoming from Fourth Estate/HarperCollins (in North America), and Simon & Schuster (in the U.K.). Slightly more inchoate are *Interminable Shrieks,* his opera for children, and *Beelzebubba,* a country-and-western reworking of Faust.

Jason Roeder lives in Somerville, Massachusetts.

Jim Ruland works at an L.A. ad agency and is a veteran of the U.S. Navy.

Tom Ruprecht is a writer for *The Late Show with David Letterman.* His work has also appeared in the *New York Times,* the *Wall Street Journal,* and *GQ.* If it's okay with the other contributors, he'd like to dedicate this book to his family.

Brian Sack is interested in human emotions.

Jessica Sedgewick graduated from Princeton University in 1998 and currently lives in Pittsburgh. She is finishing her first novel.

Kevin Shay writes fiction, plays, humor, and Perl code. He lives in Brooklyn, where he is working on a novel and developing a web site at staggernation.com.

Jim Stallard grew up in Missouri and now lives in Brooklyn. He writes about science in his day job. He worked in the Supreme Court from 1985–1987 and played many times on the building's basketball court, which does indeed exist.

Amy L. Stender received her amazing sea-monkey kit as a birthday present from one of her co-workers. Her sea-monkeys grew large enough to be called "gross," then died of starvation. She is a Vermonter.

Aaron Stoker-Ring lives in Brooklyn with his wife Clare. He writes humor for all media.

Jake Swearingen is a college student at the University of Arkansas who makes meals out of condiments, novels out of *TV Guide*s, and a life out of the accumulation of seconds.

Jenny Traig is the author of *Judaikitsch* and *Crafty Girl* (both from Chronicle Books). She has a Ph.D. from Brandeis University, but no formal dance experience.

Paul Tullis, currently residing in Hollywood, California, is occasionally employed in the culture industry. This is the fifth book to publish his writing, but not the first.

J. M. Tyree has worked as a gas-station attendant, house painter, filing clerk, and sub-sub-librarian. He was an occasional correspondent for the late *Three Weeks.*

Stuart Wade is a writer and publicist who lives in Austin, Texas.

Joshua Watson lives and works in New York City.

Adam C. Weitz produces music under the name "Phofo." He is a trial attorney.

R. J. White lives and works in Ann Arbor, Michigan, where he co-wrote this piece back in 1999 while he was supposed to be working. If he doesn't screw things up, he should be married to Laura by the time you are holding this very book in your hands. He enjoys Neil Diamond without irony.

Blake Wirht hails from the Great Central Valley of California but now lives in Los Angeles. His current project is a screenplay that has less to do with cats than it really should.